DESTINY'S SONG

AUDREY FAYE

COPYRIGHT

DEDICATION

For Robb, who has heard me sing.

"We are but flotsam—vestiges of fluff on a galactic sea. It is only in knowing this that we can truly learn how to swim."

Incendio Vargas, Poet Laureate, Aurelius II

"YO, KISH."

I tried to resist the urge to strangle the guy calling my name. I was two seconds away from the door to my pod, a good mug of Tee's homebrew, and a bath in my entire water ration for the month. I turned to face the spike-haired teenager who had put his life between me and domestic bliss. "You want to die, Zee?"

Zane Lightbody, baby brother of my roommate and general all-around pest, blinked hard. "Singers aren't supposed to kill people."

KarmaCorp has all kinds of rules for its personnel. I'm not well known for following them. "I could make an exception."

"You won't." He looked almost sure. "Tee would be mad."

Tyra got mad about as often as the head of the Inter-planetary Federated Commonwealth Council farted on vidscreen. "Is there a reason you're here, or can I strangle you now and leave you for compost?"

"Human bones go straight to the Growers, you know that. They need the calcium for mineralizing their soil mixes."

Only a dumb sixteen-year-old space brat lectures a would-be killer on the proper disposal of his body parts. I reached for the thumb-swipe on my pod door. "Go away, Zane. I'll see you Sunday at dinner." He and Tyra came from the most normal family in the galaxy. His dad made fried fish and rice every Sunday, and the whole family gathered at skydusk to eat and chat and catch up on each other's lives.

And ever since the first week of trainee school when I'd been summarily dumped into a co-pod with one Tyra Lightbody, my presence was expected at Sunday dinner.

His eyes lit. "Cool—Mom will be really jazzed you're back." He clicked his heels together, activating the old-school air-wheels that had somehow not yet been outlawed in the walkways. "Catch you later. Tell Tee I said hi."

She could probably hear that for herself—her baby brother was seriously loud. I swiped a grimy thumb across the security pad, grateful when the door opened without complaining. It had been randomly denying us entry for months, and neither of us had the spare change to cough up for a tech. Besides, beating on the door usually worked. Eventually.

"Hey, Kish. Welcome home." The cheerful voice

greeted me from the depths of our small pod. "Close the door gently, I've got bread rising."

I felt the grime and weariness of the trip start to lift off my shoulders. It had taken Tee a good six months after we'd moved in together to convince me to try her home-baked bread—it was made with microbes, for freak's sake. But something about the smell of those microbes cooking in the little box her dad had wired together as a home-leaving gift had eventually convinced me to live danger-ously. I've been eating weird shit with microbes in it ever since.

I reached into my travel bag, inhaling the happy smells of yeast and friendship. "Get that stuff cooking—I brought you a present."

Her neatly coiffed head peeked around the corner that divided our tiny kitchen from the rest of the podspace. "Oooh, what?"

She had a little kid's love of treats and surprises. I held out the slightly squished tube, a lot worse for the wear after four days traveling inside one of my packed gravboots. "I brought you butter."

She squealed like a teenager at a vid concert. "The real stuff—are you serious? It must have cost two cycles' pay."

More than that, but I wasn't going to dampen her exuberance. "I figure there's enough there to take some to your dad, too." His fried fish was always good, but I'd had it a couple of times done up with real butter, and it had damn near put me into a coma.

"He'll be over the moon." She took the tube with

reverent hands. "We're going to totally pig out first, though. Bread will be ready in an hour, so go get clean."

Tee's my best friend in the universe, but she can also be bossy as hell. "Yes, Mom."

"Whatever." She rolled her eyes and set down the butter, slinging herself into one of the ancient gel-chairs we called furnishings. "Stay grunge, see if I care. How'd the assignment go?"

The way they always went. Tricky with a helping of "oh, shit" on top. "When I got there, half the biome was ready to burn someone else at the stake." And that had been the saner half of the population. "It got worse while I was en route, apparently." When I'd left, it had just been your garden-variety revolt under way.

"Ouch." She shook her head, commiserating. "They never call you guys in fast enough."

All Fixers get sent into tough situations, but Singers have a special affinity for bringing people into harmony— it's one of the things our Talent does best. And Singers with wide vocal ranges get sent into situations where the parties are particularly far apart. I sighed. "In this case, I'm not sure there was anyone law-abiding enough left to make the call." A passing ship had radioed in the initial alert.

"A hard one, huh?" Tee's voice was full of sympathy.

"It went fine—it was just exhausting." When the people involved started kilometers apart on their desires, it was damned hard work to find the harmonics that would draw them together, and even more work to sustain those notes while stubborn heads and chakras contemplated the inevitable.

Tee has the personality for that kind of work—she's a born mediator. Me, I just try to outlast the idiots. I don't have much choice. Talents don't give a shit about personalities or anything else—they manifest wherever they damn well please. "I had to hold the final notes for almost two days."

She murmured all the right wordless things.

I leaned back, soaking in the satisfaction of telling a tale of woe to someone who really knew how to commiserate. "And then the jerk-off guy flying the tin can that brought me home missed his bounce by about ten nanos and put us through some really ugly negative-G acrobatics." Which had been hell on my aching lungs. The exhausted muscles between my ribs had been ready to decapitate the pilot where he sat. "I probably shouldn't have yelled at him." He'd totally deserved it, but my larynx didn't.

Tee winced. "Aww, your poor throat." She reached for a tiny bottle of aqua-blue liquid sitting on a nearby shelf. "Here, swallow a few drops of that when you go to bed tonight."

I'd do it in a heartbeat—her brews were magic. "Done, thanks. Got anything for my ribs?"

She smiled. "A good night's sleep."

That sounded seriously decent too. I closed my eyes, enjoying a moment of companionable silence. Tee knows when to talk and when to shut up, and I've always loved her for it. On a mining rock, the noise never stops. Silence was one of the first gifts KarmaCorp delivered to me. After that, the gifts had landed with more strings attached.

"Don't get too comfortable," said my roommate quietly.

I didn't like the sound of that. I squinted one eye open. "What's up?"

She shrugged. "Bean's been trying to reach you."

Yikes. The boss lady's assistant. They hadn't even let me get through Review yet, the mandatory tune-up every Fixer was subjected to when she came off a job—Yesenia insisted on it. They'd check to see that my vocals hadn't developed any strange wobbles while I'd been yelling at the shithead space pilot.

I could have told them not to bother, but nobody disobeyed the edicts of Yesenia Mayes, whether they agreed with her or not. The woman ran the KarmaCorp presence in this corner of the Commonwealth with a strict and arrogant fist—but based on the stories I'd heard from Fixers in other parts of the galaxy, she also ran a tight ship free of most of the crap that has infected bureaucracies since time began. And while I'd never seen her show mercy, I'd never seen her be overtly cruel, either —and a mining-asteroid brat like me has a pretty good nose for such things.

However, none of that made her any less scary.

"Yo, Earth to Kish."

I snorted. Neither of us has ever been anywhere near the planet that gave birth to our ancestors out of some sort of primordial ooze. "I'm still here. And since it's about to be after hours, I vote you raid your brew stash."

She grinned. "What brew stash?"

I rolled my eyes. "What, you got all legal and proper while I was gone?" Not likely. Tee is sweet and gentle and a goddess because she puts up with me, but she's not as much of a pushover as she looks. She flexes the rules with the best of us, and then bats her flirty brown eyes at the people in charge and generally manages to stay out of trouble. It's hard to hate her for it, though—she's too damn nice. Always has been, even in the early days of trainee school when I'd been ready to chew nails and hated everyone who breathed within a hundred meters of me.

My first friend.

I took the clear glass of light purple brew she handed my way and sighed in deep contentment. It was good to be home.

2

"HEY, KISH—WELCOME BACK." The cheerful face of Yesenia's assistant peered out from my tablet. "You got time to go through a few things?"

I had a belly full of Tee's homemade bread and the yogurt she made from coconut milk and hoarded like gold bars. Even the boss couldn't rock me out of my happy lassitude. "Sure thing." I swung my feet up on a gel-stool and settled in. Chats with Bean were never brief. I grinned at one of the people I liked best in the galaxy. "Any of the new trainees call you Lucy yet?"

Yesenia's executive assistant and right hand had been born Lucinda Coffey. Her grandmothers and the occasional dumb trainee called her Lucy—the rest of the Commonwealth called her Bean.

She winced. "Not yet."

Whoever did would get a friendly warning. After that, they'd get a visit. Fixers took care of their own, and Bean was as universally loved as the drink she'd named herself after. Which was a fair feat when you were often the messenger for a woman who ate small children for breakfast and reduced grown men to quivering puddles frequently enough that every bartender on Stardust Prime recognized the symptoms.

I eyed my tablet, vaguely embarrassed to be wool-gathering. "You got my report, yeah?" I'd filed it two minutes before docking, and written it in the ten minutes before that.

"Got it." Bean nodded solemnly. "It's a little sparse."

More than a little. "I'm economical with my words."

"I'll pass that along to Yesenia if she has concerns."

I snorted, knowing that was an entirely idle threat, at least in my case. "I brought you back some flowers." Bean had an unreasonable fondness for things that died in less than a week, and the rebellious biome had been lousy with a bunch of varieties I'd never seen.

Her entire face softened. "Zane delivered them a few minutes ago, thank you."

Hopefully Tee's baby brother hadn't smushed them against more than a few walls on his way. "Did they arrive in one piece?"

She chuckled. "Mostly."

Damn, I needed a better delivery service.

"So hey, can I get you to drop in on a trainee class while you're here?" Her voice was almost pleading. "You don't have to give a talk or anything, just do a question-and-answer session. Let them see a real, live Singer in the flesh."

Poor Bean had the thankless job of trying to keep

trainee school from entirely sucking. "Haven't I already done that twice this rotation?"

"Different class. This is the third-years—they're harder to impress."

And past the trauma of being yanked away from home, which was hard, even for the ones who were willing. I hadn't been one of the willing ones, which was why Bean often sent me to visit the youngest classes. "What am I supposed to do to entertain them, Andalusian tap dance?"

She grinned. "Just be yourself. You can wow them with your command presence and steady temperament."

I laughed. We both knew I'd missed the lines where those were handed out.

Her head tilted a little to the left. "Remember what a big deal it was when one of the Fixers came to your class fresh off an assignment?"

That was playing dirty. I'd been eleven the first time it had happened, still coated in several layers of mining-brat grime and looking for a way back home. The woman who'd come to visit with us had been a Dancer, and by the time she'd left, something far less putrid and home-sick had been running through my veins. "I'm not going to Sing for them."

Bean snorted. "That's what you always say."

It's what I always meant. I had no willpower against shiny eyes and wistful faces, grimy or not. "Just let me know when to be there."

"I will." She held a couple of fingers up to her screen cam. "Thanks."

I had no willpower against kind hearts, either. "Is that all you need?" It was exactly an hour after breakfast, but I felt a nap coming on. Travel lag is such a strange beast.

"Nope." Bean sounded apologetic. "I have the briefing file for your new assignment. Sending it now."

I tapped on the small, blinking folder on my screen, shaking my head at the name emblazoned across the top. Lakisha Drinkwater—after twenty-five years, you'd think it would feel like mine. It was a nod to two of the many heritages flowing in the mongrel blood of my adoptive family, and an overlong mouthful of a name nobody ever bothered to use. Those who know me well call me Kish. Everyone else calls me Singer, because that's my function in the universe. What they call me behind my back is their problem. Singers don't tend to make a lot of friends—people get a bit twitchy when you can open your mouth, sing a note or two, and screw with their lives.

Or so says the mythology Yesenia works hard to feed, anyhow. She wants the Fixers respected—and in the language she understands, that means she wants us feared.

I spread the folder's contents out on my screen, scanning for the data that mattered. As usual, KarmaCorp buried the important stuff in a sea of background material I could have easily looked up for myself on the Google-Plex. My eyes hit the first critical piece of information and paused. "Where the hell's Bromelain III?" I knew most of the Federation planets in this quadrant. "Don't tell me I have to ride in a sleep bucket." I'd only done cryo-travel once and I'd hated every oblivious second of it.

"Nope. It's only six days away. One of the outpost colonies."

That could mean anything from lawless to fourth generation and ready to join the Federated Commonwealth as a grown-up. It also explained why I'd never heard of them. Fixers rarely got sent to the colony planets —not enough happened there that could shake the galaxy's core. They were more the province of the Anthros. The rest of us got held firmly behind the borders that kept the inner planets sheltered and safe, and the colonies free to innovate and find their own way until they got stable enough to join the club.

I scanned a few more lines and files—and then two words in red registered. "Get out." I squinted at Bean's tiny face in the top corner of my tablet. "Why the heck is this 'Ears Only'?"

"You know I can't answer that."

I knew she wasn't supposed to, but Bean usually managed to work around the rules when it mattered.

I enlarged the video app to full-screen. "What's going on?"

"Can't tell you." She looked apologetic and a little squirmy. "I don't actually know all the details. Yesenia can see you any time this afternoon."

A squirmy Bean was disturbing—Yesenia willing to fit me into her schedule was terrifying. "When's a good slot?"

Her eyes scanned something that I assumed was the

boss lady's calendar. "How about right after lunch?" She glanced sideways and spoke under her breath. "She's been on a bit of a tear lately."

I snorted. "When isn't she?"

Bean choked on a laugh. "Gotta run, I hear the next meeting arriving. Thanks again for the flowers."

Some people were really easy to please. "No big. See you this aft." I signed off and flipped my tablet over to GooglePlex mode. Time to do some digging on Bromelain III, and not in the nice, manicured fields of the KarmaCorp briefing materials.

3

I YAWNED as I crossed the threshold into the offices of the woman who ran KarmaCorp in this part of the galaxy. Should have stopped for some caffeine. Dealing with Yesenia was tricky enough without the loggy brain that always hit me after long-haul space flights and late-morning naps. "Afternoon, Bean."

The small, lithe woman behind the desk rolled back the balance ball she used as a chair and bounced up. Her dreads bobbed madly as she closed the distance and placed a big, hard kiss on my cheek. "Kish! You look like hell. Didn't Tyra feed you and make you take a nap?"

I grinned, well used to the unnecessary mothering. "She did. I saved a piece of bread for you." I dug in my bag to rescue it before it turned to crumbs.

Bean opened a corner of the small container and inhaled deeply—and then her eyes shot open. "You got real butter?"

"Ssh." I laughed, quietly. "You want to share that with half the habitat?"

She tore off the lid and popped a good chunk of it into her mouth. "Nope." She chewed twice and closed her eyes, humming a note of quiet bliss.

That was better for my loggy brain than caffeine. "Boss lady ready for me?"

Bean waved her hand vaguely in the direction of Yesenia's inner sanctum.

I took that as invitation and stepped toward the door. It slid open moments before I got there. Yesenia came around her gleaming desk, hand out in royal greeting. "Welcome back, Journeywoman Drinkwater."

The urge to tweak her was irresistible. "Gods, Yesenia—when are you going to call me Kish like the rest of the solar system?"

Her eyes glinted sharp steel. "I very rarely seek to be like the rest of the solar system."

Truer words were never said—and I wasn't dumb enough to mess with the steel in her eyes twice. "I hear you have a new assignment for me."

"Always straight to business." She sighed, which froze me in my boots. "I used to be like you, mind always focused from one assignment to the next."

Yesenia was a Fixer legend, one of the few Travelers who'd done her stint and could still talk in complete sentences. I didn't know whether she started out tough as nails, but she'd certainly finished that way. Regret wasn't in her vocabulary. I stepped very carefully, on high alert for exploding space debris. "KarmaCorp trains us to focus."

"Yes, we do." Something in her demeanor shifted. "And you do it very well, Lakisha—I never meant to suggest otherwise. What do you know of your next assignment?"

I knew that a backwoods planet needed a Fixer—and I knew the situation had somehow merited enough attention to get labeled high security. "The file said 'Ears Only.'"

"It did." She waited a long moment, her face the impassive mask that could start a miscreant babbling in two seconds flat. "Lucinda didn't fill you in any further?"

I didn't throw friends under mining carts, and this time, Bean had known very little. "She told me Bromelain III was an outpost colony."

Yesenia raised an unimpressed eyebrow. "A little weak on your quadrant geography, are you?"

There was no point trying to explain standard human weakness to a woman who had none. "I've learned a little more since I got the file."

She tapped her fingers on a tablet that could probably turn mine into a pile of metal shards without even trying hard. "Other than a quick review while you were in contact with Lucinda this morning, I have no record of you accessing the briefing materials."

Knowing KarmaCorp tracked my every move was far less annoying than having it shoved in my face. "You might look at the records of my GooglePlex activity since then—I'm sure those will be more informative."

My prickly tone had Yesenia's eyebrow sliding up again, more dangerously this time. She took a seat in a narrow, angular chair in front of her desk and gestured to its twin. "Sit."

I didn't want to, but that was a piss-poor battle to pick. I was a grown-up now, not a fourth-year trainee who'd been caught greasing hatch locks. I made myself as comfortable as possible in a chair that clearly didn't want people sitting on it for long. "These are new."

"They are indeed." Her face gave nothing away.

I was too damn travel lagged and grouchy to keep my best manners in place. "If you put a bunch of these in the detention pod, trainees would probably be a lot better behaved."

"I'll take it under advisement."

It was way past time to stop talking about the furniture. "Intel on Bromelain III is sparse. Good climate, large grasslands sustaining the oxygen levels." Which mattered because people locked up in astrosuits all day long got really jumpy. BroThree, as the locals called it, was probably a pretty mellow place compared to my last assignment. "Eligible for Federated planet status soon." Which was a big deal, and the only clue I'd found about why I might be headed that way. Federation status was the doorway into the inner circle of power, governance, and everything else that mattered in the galaxy—at least according to the people already in there.

My boss was doing an excellent imitation of a statue. An impatient and possibly displeased one.

I tried to think what else I'd dug up that might

matter. "Not much chatter on the sim waves. Inheritor planet, so governance is pretty straightforward."

"Ah." Yesenia leaned forward, interrupting my spiel. Statue awakened. "Tell me what you learned about the Lovatts."

Other than knowing they were the family that ran the place, not much. I wondered what I'd missed. "Standard Inheritor structure—ruling title passes to the most-suited child, as voted on by the council and citizens."

She nodded her head once and looked marginally less displeased. "Did you know that in Earth-based feudal societies, it was the firstborn male child who inherited?"

I was no Anthro, but that sounded dumb as rocks. "Doesn't that just provide incentive for the firstborn to end up dead?"

"Indeed."

My brain was sending high-alert signals again. There was something going on here besides a history lesson. "Is the Inheritor Elect in danger?" That was an unusual assignment for a Singer, but I'd had stranger.

"Not at all." Yesenia's fingers tapped a riff on her knee. "Devan Lovatt was chosen most suited for leadership at the council plenarium last year. The vote was unanimous."

I shifted gingerly in the chair. "So he's the heir apparent."

"It wasn't a difficult vote—his sisters have made clear that they aren't interested."

As I'd learned at ten years old, lack of interest doesn't

always get you off the hook. "Do they show any aptitude?"

Yesenia inclined her head, teacher to adequately bright student. "One shows significant talent with solar mechanics, and the other is pregnant with her fourth child and writes a well-respected series of vidbooks for children."

"A family with varied skills." And ones that didn't provide a lot of clues about why KarmaCorp was interested in the political machinations of a backwater colony. "I assume the sister with engineering skills is on a ship somewhere." Good solar mechanics were literally worth their bodyweight in gold.

"She is, for the past two years now. Her mentors report admirable progress."

And somewhere in there might lie the reason that a Fixer was being sent to an outpost colony. Any genes that could produce solar mechanics would have earned themselves a place on KarmaCorp's radar. I didn't ask for details—there was no chance in any planet's hells that I'd get an answer, and I didn't really want one. Commonwealth politics were as convoluted and labyrinthine as it got. I was just a Singer who did what I was told, and very glad to keep it that way.

Time to get the down low on my assignment and get out of here. "Forgive my lack of patience, Director, but why are you sending me to Bromelain III?"

"You'll be observing Devan Lovatt."

I raised an eyebrow of my own, thoroughly confused.

Fixers didn't generally get sent to babysit, even for royalty.

Yesenia's hands played that riff on her knee again. "And a young woman by the name of Janelle Brooker."

Sometimes notes sound bad even before they're played. "And who would she be, exactly?"

"She's the middle daughter of another well-respected colony family." The boss lady's game face did nothing to calm my gut. "The Brookers can trace their roots all the way back to the grain fields of Saskatchewan."

That bit of geography I did know. Canada hadn't been the first of Earth's countries into space, but they'd been one of the last left with water and land that could grow things, and that had fueled their colonization of half the star system. A country of pioneers used to cold and isolation, they'd had the right DNA for space exploration. That made the Brookers at least minor relations to galactic royalty, and Yesenia wanted to make sure I knew it.

This was getting stinkier than a compost droid. We had two young people on some backwoods space rock, and either their family connections or some situation they'd managed to get tangled up in had qualified them for a high-security KarmaCorp intervention. "Did they get themselves into something sticky?"

"In a manner of speaking."

I sat quietly, not at all sure I wanted to hear what came next.

"Our astrologers believe the two are compatible and intended to marry."

I tried not to gape, shocked to the core that they'd pointed a StarReader at two kids on some outpost planet. Astrologers were a credit a dozen all over the galaxy, but KarmaCorp employed the ones who ended up right most of the time—and there weren't nearly enough of them. They were the company's most valuable commodity. "What, I'm supposed to keep the two of them out of trouble before the wedding?"

"No. Apparently the two parties are not yet convinced of their future together."

That was crazy. "Nobody argues with a KarmaCorp StarReader."

Yesenia's lips pursed. "They aren't to be told. No one is. That information will not leave this office."

That was even crazier.

She eyed me with a look that regularly froze the blood of people two decades my senior. "That directive comes from the highest levels, and you will comply with it, Journeywoman."

That could only mean StarReader edict. One that likely had far more tentacles than a simple marriage on some boondocks colony. I grimaced—and then the other shoe landed, the whole reason a Singer was being pulled into this mess. To create harmony where none existed. "No. No way."

Yesenia's eyebrows warned of impending death should I choose to keep up my foolish babble.

The knots in my gut cowered and kept talking anyhow. "That's insane." And far, far worse than babysitting.

"That is for others to decide." She was Yesenia Mayes in full throttle now, and no one would dare to cross her. "You will do your job, Singer, and you will do it with all the skill, talent, and training at your disposal."

Of course I would—there was never any other choice. Fixers did what we were told.

But sweet holy shit. I was being sent off to a backwater rock—to be a matchmaker.

4

I'D FORGOTTEN how thirteen-year-old girls were such an odd mix of lingering child and the adults they would one day become. No boys in this class, but that wasn't a surprise—Fixer Talents most often manifested in girls, especially at this age.

I'd campaigned hard to do this in the student lounge, which was a mess of gel-chairs, holo-covered walls, and excellent snacks, but I'd been overruled. Which sucked, because my stomach was kicking up a fuss about the lack of decent sustenance I'd sent its direction recently.

The trainees were impressively still under my gaze. They were older than the last class I'd talked to—less wiggly, less wet behind the ears, and less obviously impressed by my presence in their midst. Good. Maybe their questions would be a little less awestruck, too. "Well, I could stand up here and say a bunch of stuff about Fixers and the important work we do, but I bet you've heard it all before." And I'd probably find it hard to say with a straight face when my next assignment involved adjusting some guy's hormones so that his dick pointed the right way.

Hands shot up all over the room. I picked a waving one at random.

The girl who stood up was as wide as she was tall, and every inch of it was clearly muscle. "Is being a Fixer dangerous?"

She obviously hoped the answer was yes. "It can be, but danger takes a lot of different forms. And usually means we didn't do our job right." Or someone higher up the chain hadn't, but thirteen-year-olds didn't want to hear about bureaucratic fuck-ups.

"I thought Fixers didn't make mistakes." A girl down in front looked fairly distressed about that possibility.

I recognized her elfin looks—she came from one of the most overprotected families in the quadrant. Unfortunately, they also produced a lot of kids with Talent. "Everyone makes mistakes, and those of us with Talent sometimes make the biggest ones. That's why it's important to work on your judgment, too."

The elf frowned. "How do we do that?"

In her family, I had no idea—probably by running away from home. "You make decisions every day, right?" In her case, not very big ones, but still. "You decide what to eat, what to wear, who to be nice to, who to share your lunch with."

She looked totally confused.

This kid would last ten minutes on a mining rock, and someday she might get sent there. I sighed—I was a

Fixer, not a nanny. "Basically, you practice. You notice when you make smart decisions and when you make dumb ones, and you try to get better."

Her eyes crossed. "But I thought we're supposed to do what we're told."

We were, and I'd just been reminded of that in no uncertain terms. "Absolutely. Fixer assignments are decided with great care and planning and access to a lot of information that we don't have." So far, I was spouting the company manual, but it was time to change that up a little. I glanced over at the wall where the teacher stood, looking a little bored. "But there are good reasons that KarmaCorp puts Fixers on the ground. We do *what* we're told, but we have a lot of freedom to decide *how* we do it." Something some of us took more advantage of than others.

The teacher wasn't looking bored anymore—but she hadn't stopped me, either. And every pair of trainee eyes in the room was riveted.

Which left me trying to explain a line I hadn't remotely understood at thirteen. "Everything has resonance, energy—right? We have the Talent to tap into that energy, to shape it." Thanks to a few Saskatchewan farmers with pretty interesting genetics that had been seeded out into space. "That can't be done from an office. Energy needs to be *felt*, and every person in KarmaCorp knows it. That's our job."

I could Sing however I wanted—so long as I got the job done. And complied with KarmaCorp's very long ethics manual, but that was a different conversation, and one plenty of other people would be having with the trainees. I wasn't here to tell them about the limits. I was here to tell them how to find enough freedom to stay sane—the wiggle room that had allowed a mining brat to do the job with dignity and pride. Elf girl was still looking confused, but several other heads were nodding. Idea planted. Time to head back to safer ground. "Any more questions?"

A girl with dark skin and an appealing grin bounced up next. "I heard your next assignment is to an outpost colony."

She said the last two words with the light disdain of a kid who'd been born on one of the Commonwealth's inner planets. "It is." Which was probably a secret, but if the thirteen-year-olds already knew, not a very well-kept one.

The grin ratcheted up a notch. "What are you going to do there?"

That *was* a secret, and I was pretty damn sure Yesenia kept trainees out of the Ears Only files. "Whatever is necessary to help alignment and the flow of good energy in the galaxy."

The questioner scowled, not at all impressed with being quoted KarmaCorp's mission statement. "A colony planet doesn't sound very important."

Definitely inner-planet born. "I bet fixing Andrew Takli's fear of small spaces didn't sound very important either." Even a first-year trainee would know the story of the eight-year-old boy who had gone on to develop modern cryo-travel. They would have also heard the horror stories of Fixers who had failed in something simple they'd been sent to do and put whole cultures into tailspin. "Even the smallest assignment can have vast ripples out into the universe."

Which didn't make me any happier about being sent off to get two people all hot for each other, but it would keep me doing my job.

My interrogator wasn't done. Her head cocked to the side, thinking. "Do you *know* why your new assignment is important?"

"No."

The teacher shifted on the wall.

I held the kid's gaze. They wanted me to talk about what it was like to be a real-live Fixer, and that included flying blind more often than not.

The girl met my gaze, her dark eyes thoughtful. "How come they don't tell us?"

The long answer would bore her to tears—the one about the very delicate balance of trust and autonomy that lived at KarmaCorp's core and helped sustain a galaxy with more decency, generosity, and happiness than had ever been seen in human history. So I went with the short one. "We'd have to be in meetings all day and read reports until our eyes bled."

Groans rose up all over the room. I grinned. "We're people of action, right?" And the price for that sometimes included not understanding why we acted. I'd try to remember that while I was encouraging two boondocks colonists to hop into each other's pants.

I looked around for another question and picked a nondescript girl with sharp, savvy eyes.

She stayed seated and spoke in a clear voice full of bells. Definitely a Singer. "What's the hardest part about being a Fixer?"

I blinked. Most trainees didn't see past the glisten and gloss for years yet. "Working in the field alone, I think. Having to make hard decisions without really knowing what the best answer is." And knowing that if you screwed up, people died and communities failed and doorways into important futures slammed closed.

The savvy eyes had a follow-up. "And what's the best part?"

I grinned. "Working in the field alone."

She grinned back and nodded appreciatively.

That one was going places. I looked around, grateful that the waving hands were diminishing, and nodded at a slender arm in the back corner. A girl with bright orange hair slid to her feet with the kind of grace that could only belong to a Dancer. "Do you think they'll find another Traveler soon?"

I sure as hell hoped not. Talent was rough on all of us, but Singers and Dancers and Growers generally lived to tell their tales and scare small children in the pod nurseries. Shamans had it harder because they played with the most woo energies—the ones that came with very few rules and pissy manners. But the Travelers were gifted with all our Talents *and* the ability to move through space and time. They were rare, extremely coveted, and had really short life expectancies.

KarmaCorp hunted for Travelers in every corner of the galaxy, and in my lifetime, there had been three. I looked at the girl who had asked the question and sent me woolgathering. "No idea."

I saw a few eyes in the class sidle toward a student in the back. She was elegant ice, sitting chill and still with a snooty look on her face.

We didn't need an introduction. Tatiana Mayes, only progeny of Yesenia Mayes and headed straight for the Fixer elite ever since she'd been old enough to get her thumb into her mouth. If she was a Traveler, it hadn't manifested yet—but the possibility had already earned her a world of privilege, hatred, and overprotected hovering.

This was the first time we'd actually come face-to-face. I looked at her square on, curious to see what she was made of.

Two golden eyes met mine, gaze even and registering slightly bored.

I let the tiniest smile show, impressed, despite my best intentions. Yesenia's cub had some backbone.

Slowly, she raised her right hand.

I was pretty sure there wasn't anything about Fixing, KarmaCorp, or the Federated Commonwealth of Planets that she didn't already know. Yesenia would have sent her spawn out into the world impeccably prepared.

Tatiana was still waiting, the bored ice queen with her hand up. And more eyes in the room were turning to watch. I raised an eyebrow slightly and engaged the battle, because whatever else this was, it was a challenge. "You have a question, Trainee Mayes?"

She acknowledged my first thrust with the barest flicker of a smile.

She wasn't surprised that I knew who she was, but she was impressed that I'd laid it out there—or at least that's what I took from the small flicker. I waited for her question.

Her eyes slid left for a brief moment, over to the non-assuming girl in blue who had asked the smartest question of the day so far—and got a quick, reassuring glance in return.

Ah, so that was the lay of the land. The cub had a friend. I found myself glad of it. Fixers without friends didn't last long, even if they'd been born into Karma-Corp's bosom.

Tatiana breathed in like one of the dolphins on Xanatos, slow and liquid and taking all the time in the world, as if oxygen was a small, permitted luxury instead of the stuff of life. "What is it like working for my mother?"

Youch. There was no way to answer that and come out without scratches.

I watched as the quiet girl in blue grinned, acknowledging the play.

I didn't mind a few scratches—and I liked Tatiana more than I'd expected to. I waited a moment and then gave her the respect of an honest answer. "I imagine it's easier than being her daughter."

The ice queen melted for just a moment, and I saw a

kid with golden eyes who knew she lived in a golden cage —and planned to get out one day.

My heart answered in an instant. I hoped she made it.

Which is the kind of thing you absolutely don't want to think as a loyal employee of KarmaCorp, or as someone who's ever caught a glimpse of Yesenia Mayes in a temper. A woman who could shred fifteen grown men over delays in interplanetary shipping schedules wasn't anyone to mess with, ever. I broke eye contact with Tatiana, cursing whatever momentary impulse had made me stupid.

And saw Yesenia, standing just inside the far left door. She saw me looking, bowed her head slightly, and slid out as silently as she had come in.

I shivered. The woman never missed anything.

Tatiana was back in her snooty, bored pose, the one I suspected she wore like a comfortable second skin—but I wasn't convinced that she missed much either.

And I was a tired Fixer about to head off-planet again who didn't need any more crap to land. I scanned my audience one more time, using that command presence I didn't generally have to suggest that question period was done. "Anyone else?"

A hand shot up on the far right, and a girl with bright red hair bounced up after it.

She looked enough like my friend Iggy that I capitulated. "Yes?"

She flashed the smile of a breezy sprite who never sat

still for long. "Can you show us how a Singer works? Please?"

It was the "please" that did me in. And the crystal-clear memory that I'd been the kid asking that exact same question once.

I hadn't known how to sit still for long back then either.

Something quick, and then I'd get the hell out. I looked around the lecture pod again, seeking an appropriately innocuous experiment. By third year, these girls would be old hands at controlling their Talents. They'd be learning the subtler and more important powers of observation.

The red-headed sprite's hand flew up again. "What are you doing?"

I wasn't used to working out loud, but that was the whole point of being here. "I'm assessing crowd factors. Singers don't just have voices—we have eyes, too, and smart Fixers don't use their Talent until they have to." Less paperwork that way.

The girl studied her classmates with sharp interest. "What do you see when you look at us?"

More than I'd ever let her know, but I could run through the basics. "You're far less restless than the last trainee class I visited."

She wrinkled her nose. "They were probably just tadpoles."

Apparently, the youngest trainee cohort was never going to escape that nickname. "Perhaps. Youth is one reason for people to squirm, but there are others. They might lack discipline, or they might not feel a part of the group, or they might not like what they're hearing from whoever is speaking. Those are all useful things for a Fixer to know."

There were a couple in the class who were getting restless right now. I glanced at the teacher, knowing I'd have been one of them. Her eyes were quietly traveling her students, collecting data, just like I'd been doing. Good—she wasn't one of the ones marking time until retirement, then.

Probably not a surprise with Yesenia's daughter in the room.

Which was a good reminder to tread very carefully with my little demonstration. I let my eyes flow over the trainees one more time, noting the seating pattern. The girls had organized themselves in small clumps, but I didn't know if that was teacher or trainee choice.

Mapping the basic social dynamics seemed like an innocuous enough experiment. I sought out a couple of the brighter pairs of eyes. "I see that you've seated your-selves into some interesting groupings." I held up a palm to forestall anyone answering the question I hadn't actu-ally asked. "That's something you'll see in many social settings, and it can give you important clues to work with."

A girl in the back with temp face tats much like Tee's spoke up for the first time. "So it can tell you who's important in the group, stuff like that?"

I raised an eyebrow. If I read her right, she was trying to dig me into a hole—or at the very least, daring me to call Yesenia's progeny important. "It can. But *you* sit on your own, for example, and that's something that's hard for just my eyes to interpret. Maybe the group excludes you, or maybe you control the underground lines of power in the group and you don't want me to know."

I could see the surprised flickers of respect hit her eyes. "Or maybe I'm just a loner."

I grinned, liking her attitude. "Or maybe that."

A girl at the front turned around, voice flat. "Or maybe you just got here late, like usual."

That hadn't changed since my trainee days either. I resisted the urge to punch the by-the-rules bully in the nose—it was ten years too late to be pulling dumb stunts like that. I could, however, possibly make the same point with a little more finesse. Talents never lied, especially if you knew what to ask them.

I walked out from behind the lectern, taking a few deep, cleansing breaths as I did so. "What I'm going to do now is a simple harmonics exercise. I'll find a core resonant note for each of you in the room, and then play them against each other until I find the notes that blend best together."

A few heads were nodding—those would be the Singer trainees. They'd have learned the basics of base-note mapping already. "Then I'll look at what the Song tells me, and how that compares to what my eyes have already noticed."

Confusion replaced head nods. Finally, a hesitant hand went up over to the left. "But I thought Talents were never wrong."

I'd believed that once. "They aren't wrong, but some-times their information can be incomplete or hard to understand." And since I was no philosopher, that was as much as I was going to say on the subject. "Watch. If it's still confusing when I'm done, ask your question again."

The owner of the hesitant hand nodded and settled back down.

I started with a simple staircase of thirds, purpose-fully skipping all the pretty scales and soundings trainees were taught to open with. There was never time for that junk in the field.

I hadn't made it half a phrase before eager harmonics started joining mine. The Singer trainees, answering the question my Song asked of them. I was glad to see they weren't all sitting together. Their base notes made up a clean chord with no signs of animosity, which was good. Singers rarely ended up in open conflict with each other, but when they did, it was hell for anyone in earshot.

I also noted that none of them much liked bully girl in the front row.

Four students mapped, thirteen to go. I started randomly singing base notes that occurred with the most frequency in big populations. The girl from the front row popped on the second one. It figured—half the bureau-crats in the galaxy resonated with that note. Two others in the class registered for that one as well, and three more came up as tight harmonics.

Bully girl had a following.

Seven left. These were thirteen-year-olds, so I shifted to a minor key, looking for the kids who were playing in the lands of drama and angst. Four more fit there, and two of the Singer trainees echoed my shift, making it clear they hung out there sometimes too. I sang back a soothing message of acceptance. In another five years, most of them would have moved back out of the minor keys, but thirteen was an age to explore your shadows.

One of them sent back a quick subsonic trill of gratitude. I raised an eyebrow at their teacher in the back, surprised. That was advanced for this group. She nodded subtly. Exceptional Talent already noted.

Three left. These would be the tricky ones, and the most fun.

I shifted to chromatics, looking for the offbeat personalities, and smiled as the girl with the face tats pinged right away. Interesting, though—her base note fit in well with the Singers. We tend to attract rebels who know how to behave themselves when it matters. Or ones who would learn that one day, anyhow. I didn't expect any thirteen-year-old kid to have their shit together.

The next chromatic to hit shocked my Song to its core. Tatiana Mayes, child queen, resonated on a note I hadn't seen in years—and her base note was a trio. Two of the notes were faint yet, but they were there. Warrior, artist, and rebel, all in a tightly wrapped package of ice.

My eyes darted to the door, but Yesenia hadn't magically materialized again.

She must know. There was no way she couldn't.

Cool golden eyes intercepted mine on the return journey. The cub, pissed that I'd wandered off to check in with mommy.

I wasn't nearly dumb enough to engage that fight. I stepped back behind the lectern and cut off my Song. Time to throw the trainees a couple of interesting bones and get the heck out of town. There was far too much strangeness on the prowl this circuit home, and a smart cog knew when to duck and run.

The student with face tats had her hand up like a shot. "So now that you know all about us, what would you do? If we were like your assignment or something, and you had to get us all to cooperate?"

I'd punch bully girl in the nose, but since someone in charge hadn't done that already, I had to assume she was filling a purpose. I smiled at the class in general and hummed three quick notes.

The trainee in the back with the trills and the extra dose of Talent laughed. Everyone else stared at her or me, mystified.

Then tats girl put a hand on her belly as stomachs all over the room growled. "The heck? You made us all hungry?"

I grinned. And made my final point. "I stopped a ship's mutiny that way once." I waited for that to land. Anything can be a tool if you aim it well enough.

I left to scattered applause, whispers, and a couple of Singer trainees trying to replicate my three notes. They were missing, but not by much.

I grinned on my way out the door. Most of them would forget me in an hour, but a few were thinking. And one or two might remember something I said when they faced down an angry revolt or a power-hungry politico someday.

My version of small ripples. A gift to a pond I deeply believed in.

Not bad for an afternoon's work.

5

IT WAS TOTALLY STRANGE HAVING a sendoff while still travel lagged from my previous assignment. I eyed the contents of the lime-green beaker in my hand—it probably wasn't going to help with the travel lag any.

Sendoffs were ritual, however, and one the four of us took very seriously. You never knew when a Fixer might not return.

I looked around at the bodies draped over gel pillows on our tiny living-space floor and grinned. If I was going to die, these were definitely the people I'd want to see last. The four of us had been tight since the first week we'd arrived. The first year of trainee school had been hell, and I'd survived purely and solely because of the lunatics who had chosen to befriend the feisty, angry, blonde-haired demon child who'd been plucked out of a mining colony and everything she'd ever known and hated every molecule of the idea that she was now KarmaCorp flotsam.

I scowled and took a sip of my brew—whatever was in it was already making me maudlin. Being KarmaCorp flotsam had turned out to be a pretty decent gig.

Imogene, far better known as Iggy, poked one of her toes into my thigh. "You don't get to start brooding already, girl."

I moved my thigh out of her reach—Dancer toes are crazy strong. "I'm not brooding. Half my brain's still stuck on the tin can that brought me back here."

"Fast turnaround, huh?" Iggy reached for a Renulian grape, her contribution to the night's food. "That's what you get for being the best Singer in the quadrant."

I amused myself by watching the artwork on her face wiggle as she talked. She and Tee had been decorating each other again. "Right. That's why they're sending me to make sure a couple of healthy adults get all kissyface with each other." That was treading a fine line on the Ears Only deal, but they'd keep it quiet.

Tee's eyes danced. "They should have sent Iggy— she's got the kissyface thing totally down."

Clearly life hadn't stopped while I'd been gone on my last gig. "Romeo finally got his act together, did he?"

"Nope." Raven, our foursome's resident Shaman, grinned as she reached for the bowl of grapes. "A new guy swooped in and stole all the action."

"He did not." Iggy waggled a suggestive eyebrow. "I did the swooping, thank you very much."

I debated between grapes and chocolate-dipped chilies. "Man, I missed all the good stuff." I eyed the other two of our crew. "You guys checked him out, right?"

"Did." Raven took one of the chocolate chilies. "He's solid." She grinned at her roommate. "And full of sexy energy."

Iggy just rolled her eyes. "Like you needed to read the airwaves to figure that out."

Shamans read all kinds of shit none of the rest of us understand—but if Raven thought this guy was good people, that was about as close to a guarantee as you could get.

Tee grinned and poured more stuff into my beaker. "I just want to know if he has a brother or two."

I shook my head. "Just how many bed buddies do you need at one time?" Growers were known for their sexual appetites, but my roommate had become something of a Fixer legend in that regard. I took another sip of my drink, damn glad her hormones weren't contagious. Bed buddies were something I did sparingly and with as few complications as humanly possible.

My roommate fluttered her eyelashes and grinned, entirely unfazed by my teasing. She'd grown up with the comfort of knowing exactly who she was, and the razzing of a lowly mining brat wasn't going to change that any. I had reason to know—I'd tried pretty hard to shake her, once upon a time.

Raven picked up a bright pink beaker and toasted my direction. "So, what's your assignment location like?"

She'd phrased that carefully enough that I could answer however I liked. Shamans got Ears Only files a lot more often than the rest of us. "It's a colony planet. Info's pretty sparse."

"Hmm. Past the edges of the civilized world, huh?" She raised an eyebrow. "Want me to look?"

Shamans had ways of accessing intel that the Google-Plex had never heard of. "Nah, but thanks." It would have cost her to read the airwaves that far away, and I didn't think I needed it this time.

Raven shrugged. "Suit yourself."

Tee watched me carefully over the top of a multi-colored beaker that was making swirls as she jiggled it. "It's not like you to head into an assignment blind."

I didn't want to be heading into this one at all. "I'm supposed to make two adults with functioning hormones fall for each other—how hard can that be?"

Iggy snorted. "I had a gig like that once."

I dug back through my memory banks. "I don't remember that one."

She grinned. "You should. I came back totally juiced up and it took all three of you to drag me away from the spacer bar."

That part I remembered. Dancers got things moving, but it was hard from them to stay out of the surging energy of what they unleashed. Tee was used to swimming in the sexual energies, but for Iggy, it had been an eye-opening experience. For me, too—getting her out of that bar had seared some unforgettable images on my eyeballs. Miners aren't prudes, but we mostly do things in the dark.

Raven looked at Iggy and grinned. "I think it took you at least a week to stop zinging."

She should know—the two of them had been roommates since the beginning, same as Tee and me.

Iggy just waved a graceful arm in dismissal. "Whatever. Kish, be careful what you sing at your two lovebirds, that's all I'm saying."

There weren't all that many ways I could get into trouble—Singing just didn't have the fun side effects of the other Talents. It supposedly made us all spiritual and connected to higher powers, but I tended to leave that kind of woo to the Shamans. I Sing because I have to, because it's the way I touch the light. And even that much I generally don't say out loud.

"So." Raven had settled back with the bowl of chocolate chilies in her lap. She pitched me one, always willing to share her spicy addiction. "How'd you get the rebel biome to behave itself? Scuttlebutt says you flew back cranky."

Scuttlebutt probably used some less polite words than that. "I used the overwhelming beauty of pentatonic fifths to call them forth into cooperation and reasonableness."

"Sure you did. And then they all named their firstborn children after you and lived happily ever after." She grinned. "What really happened?"

I sighed and downed more of my lime-green swill. "I got pissed off. I tried everything I could think of to get them to even consider the other side's right to breathe air, and when that didn't work, I sang a note so bad that they all finally aligned themselves to get me to shut up."

Tee slumped over into a pillow, laughing. "You didn't tell me that part."

I hadn't put it quite that way in my report, either. "It worked."

Iggy shook her head and took a tiny bite of a chili. "Rebel."

"Am not." I waved my beaker at her, somewhat precariously. "I got the job done, and I don't think I broke a single rule doing it."

Raven nodded solemnly. "You belong to KarmaCorp, heart and soul."

She wasn't far from wrong. "I should. They made me."

"They made all of us," said Tee quietly. "We all chose this."

We had. Belonging to KarmaCorp wasn't a choice, not if you had Talent. But serving was, and we had all chosen to be active field personnel. Cogs in the great, cranking wheels of KarmaCorp's mission.

Iggy aimed a toe poke at my roommate. "What'd you put in the brew? It's making us way too serious."

Tee snorted. "Dancer toe fungus."

Raven peered at the bottom of her beaker. "I knew I shouldn't have drunk it."

"What's wrong with toe fungus?"

Iggy's words were beginning to slur a little—or my ears were. I closed my eyes a moment, letting the sounds of their conversation roll over me. A three-part harmony of sorts, a little off key, but deeply familiar. The cacophony of friendship.

I hummed a quiet, grateful note of my own and lifted my drink.

Bromelain III would come soon enough. For now, I was right where I wanted to be, toe fungus and all.

6

"YOUR PREBOARDING DRINK, SINGER."

A young attendant in blue stood before me, holding out the slimy gray cocktail that was required of every space traveler. It helped our bodies prepare for the kind of trip our genes had never meant for us to take. I took the beaker, wishing it looked half as appetizing as one of Tee's drinks.

"It will help with motion sickness and cramping."

This attendant was clearly new. "I know that, thank you. I also know it tastes like horse piss."

She smiled a little. "I wouldn't know—I've never met a horse."

She'd do fine. You had to have a sense of humor to deal with space travelers on a regular basis. We tended to be a cranky lot. "Are we boarding on time?" I didn't actually know what time that was—with the much quicker-than-usual turnaround between assignments, I'd barely managed to find some clean skinsuits and replenish my stash of reading materials.

"I believe so." The attendant smiled and took my empty glass. "If you need anything else before you board, just let me or one of my associates know."

If there was more than one of her in the vicinity, this was one of the better flight companies.

I took a look outside the viewing port at the cubecraft waiting for us, spied the maple leaf on the side, and relaxed. Budgets must be looking good if I was getting to fly with the Canucks. The Canadians were expensive, but they knew how to transport a body in reasonable comfort.

My stomach rumbled in gratitude. The low-budget cubes could be gut-wrenching, to put it mildly.

I found a spot on the wall and set my travel bag down to wait. Many of my fellow travelers did the same. A few paced, and some newbies near the boarding gate were doing the prescribed pre-flight exercises. I relaxed a notch further. No one too heavily inebriated, and no one traveling with toddlers. A group of tanned, muscled guys over in the corner were making too much noise, but hopefully they'd be at the far end of the tin can. If I could manage to get myself seated next to a couple of the businessmen glued to their tablets, so much the better.

A chirpy voice started announcing levels for boarding, and I reached down for my travel bag. Reading materials and chocolate-covered cranberries, check. One ear half tuned to the instructions, I made my way into the sea of humanity that was organizing itself into the three-line formation most efficient for cube boarding. We passed through ID and ticket checks, and then the lines split again, feeding us into nine tubes that led to various entry doors.

I tried not to think about the shapes and lines too hard—they made my brain dizzy.

A small boy a few meters up my line danced in place, fractious energy bouncing off the clear walls of the loading tube. His mother already looked harried.

I gritted my teeth. I knew enough of Tee's small relatives to know that the next four days weren't likely to improve his mood any. I also knew how little it would take to calm him—and how totally against the nit-picky KarmaCorp rule book it was to do so. Little actions could have big effects.

The boy let out a shrill and rising scream that beat a Med-pod siren for intensity, hands down.

I sighed and sang a harmonic under my breath. If word got back to Yesenia's office, I'd be scrubbing compost tubes for the next rotation, but it wasn't her eardrums on the line.

The boy quieted, taking his mother's hand.

Several people near me let out sighs of relief. I let go of the harmonic and resumed my slow shuffle forward.

A head bent over my shoulder, and a melodious voice pitched words meant for me alone. "Thank you, Singer— that was well done."

I looked up at the man in surprise. My harmonic shouldn't have been audible.

He smiled. "I have grandsons, and I know a bit about

calming them down." He held out a hand. "I'm Ralph Emerson—lovely to be traveling with you."

Ah. There were at least three Emersons working this quadrant for KarmaCorp. I took his hand and shook. "I'd say the same, but after four days on board, I probably won't like you any better than anyone else."

His laugh had the same melodious undertones as his voice. No wonder his family produced Singers. "I appreciate your... initiative." His eyes said what his words couldn't—if this got back to headquarters, it wouldn't have come from him.

I'd probably survive if it did. Technically, I was on assignment already, and arriving with my eardrums intact seemed like it should qualify as reasonable use of Talent.

I didn't want to have to argue that in Yesenia's office, however.

Whatever further conversation I might have had with Ralph was interrupted by our arrival at the boarding door. I sighed as he was directed left and I was sent right. Too bad—he'd have made a stellar travel companion. I made my way to my seat and grimaced inwardly as I finally caught sight of it. I'd been dumped in with the loud guys with muscles. No good deeds go unpunished.

I squeezed past two of them and plunked down in the tiny space of real estate that had been designated as mine for the duration of our flight. The guys shuffled around and tried to get their shoulders out of my way, with limited results. Even the Canadians designed their cube-craft seats for underweight eight-year-olds.

I saw the guy beside me taking in the logo on my skinsuit that identified me as a KarmaCorp Singer, and let him look. Fixers generally went incognito for most of their time on-planet, especially the data-gathering stages, but I pulled out the uniform for travel—it tended to encourage people to leave me alone. I'd change at Corinthian Station before I boarded my final hop to Bromelain III.

I caught a flash of a tattoo sticking out from under his skinsuit and raised an eyebrow, mildly curious in return. Space travel is this weird mix of intimacy and avoidance with people you'll never see again.

He held out his arm so I could see the stylized tat with the curvy, undulating diamond.

That was answer enough. He was a Sun Dancer, one of the crazy breed that strapped solar sails to the arms of their astrosuits and went flying with the stars. No tethers, no spotting crew, no back-up propellant tanks to get back home if their fragile sail took a hit from some space debris.

They were entirely crazy, but I'd flown a couple of dances in virtual, and it was a pretty mindblowing experience. Kind of like being one of those seeds Tee croons to, with the hairy little plumes sticking out of their heads. Flotsam in a vast universe that doesn't give a damn if you live or die, but enchants you with its beauty all the same.

I wasn't that kind of flotsam. I didn't have the freedom to throw my life away on a solar flare gone amok.

Sexy guy raised an eyebrow. "Ever met a Sun Dancer before?"

"Yeah." I pulled my brain back out of the ether. He

probably assumed my glazed eyes were fantasizing about his naked chest, which, judging from what I could see through his skinsuit, wasn't an entirely unreasonable assumption.

He offered up a grin that was less arrogant than most of his kind. "You ever flown?"

He wasn't talking about a cubesat ride. "No." I made to pull the privacy bubble around my head and then reconsidered. It was a pretty long flight, and he didn't smell like totally bad company. "I've heard it's pretty addictive, though."

"Better than sex." He laughed, as much at himself as anyone else. "Most times, anyhow."

I raised an eyebrow, amused despite myself. "That's not a great advertisement for your skills."

The guy strapped in behind us reached around and boffed my seatmate's head. "Jay, you're such a dingbat." He made overt googly eyes at me. "Come sit back here—we know how to romance a woman properly."

Their odds on romancing a Singer were approximately nil, and I figured they knew that. My seatmate, now named but not at all chastened, pushed a button to call over the serverbot. "Want anything to eat?"

Generally, I avoided making my stomach do any work in spaceflight, but the Canucks usually managed gentle landings, and my appetite was still ramped up from the heavy-grav world of my last assignment. "Sure, so long as they have something that isn't soy."

The guy behind us hooted again. "Look out, Jay—this one's high maintenance."

Somehow their juvenile antics continued to find my funny bone. I might as well enjoy them for what they were—a four-day distraction I'd never see again. "It's worse than you think, hot stuff. I don't do synth-caf, either." The fake caffeine screwed with my vocal chords, but he didn't need to know that. "I like my food real." At least, I did when I could afford it, and these days, Journeywoman wages were almost up to the task of keeping my belly happy with stuff that had swum or mooed or clucked once upon a time. Tee and her family kept us well supplied with things that had grown in actual dirt.

The mining brat had gotten totally spoiled.

Jay pulled out my arm tray and set down a plasticup. "Not soy. Not real, either—sorry, the menu doesn't run to the good stuff."

Neither should the budget of a stranger. "That wasn't an actual hint."

"I know." His smile reminded me of an overgrown teddy bear. "But it would have been fun to see your reaction."

I studied him a little more carefully. Some people slot into a round hole or a square box and you don't have to think much to figure them out. This guy was a bit of a surprise, which was a characteristic I enjoyed in people I had to sit beside for days. I picked up the cup and settled deeper into my seat. Maybe it wouldn't be an entirely horrible flight.

He glanced my direction again, eyes pulled to the logo on my skinsuit. "Is it hard?"

That was a long conversation I didn't generally have with strangers. "Is what hard?"

He thought for a minute, clearly reformulating his question. "Walking around the galaxy with so much power to change things."

That was a more nuanced question than most people asked. I gave him points for having a brain and using it, and contemplated how to answer. When I wore Karma-Corp's logo on my chest, every word I said represented the company. And people, even thoughtful ones, often carried plenty of distrust for the entity I worked for.

Three hundred years ago, a small group known as the Warriors of Karma had stopped an intergalactic war in its tracks—and held peace ransom for enough assets to keep the entity they formed independent and non-aligned ever since. People still didn't know what to make of a company born from a group of peace terrorists. We were a force to be reckoned with, and in most places, a very respected one. But that didn't always mean people liked us very much. "We have less power than most people imagine."

He raised an eyebrow. "That doesn't sound like the official company line."

It wasn't. Often, half our work got done simply because of the KarmaCorp mystique. But I was a Fixer with an annoying tendency to tell the truth. I looked at sexy guy's tat again. Maybe he'd understand better than most. "It's like your swish suit and jet packs and all that. Fancy toys, but when you're facing down bumpy solar winds, I bet you don't feel very powerful."

He raised an eyebrow. "There's a difference between power and control."

"Not for a Fixer." Control was at the heart of everything we did.

He considered that for a long moment. "That sounds sad."

It might to a guy who strapped a jet pack on his back and danced with death for entertainment. "It's better than the alternatives." Before the Warriors of Karma, most people with Talent had lived short lives full of misery and destruction.

He nodded slowly. "It must take a strong person to live with all that."

No. Just one who had finally learned to find her purpose in the inevitable. "I just do my job." And somewhere along the way, I'd learned to like it pretty well. I looked over at Jay, suddenly curious again. "What do you do when you're not trying to turn yourself into space dust?"

His grin really was appealing. "I'm an accountant."

I leaned back, amused, and shook my head. "And you think *my* life has issues?"

His laugh nearly made my seat rumble.

7

THERE'S JUST no way to travel for days on end in a tin can, even a fairly comfortable tin can, without hating the universe when you crawl out. And the final insult of thirty-six hours in the transpo ferry from Corinthian Station to the landing terminal on Bromelain III had killed any remnants of goodwill I had left. We'd stopped at seven planets en route to this one, and I'd given up trying to keep track of the flow of grumpy humanity around me.

I stepped out of the disembarking tube into the small, obnoxiously bright waiting area that served as the planet's headquarters for space travel. My legs felt like they'd picked a fight with a concrete mixer, and I let the surprisingly large number of people milling around push me toward the outer walls. Walls usually had doors somewhere, and I needed a good stretch, something heavily alcoholic, and three days of uninterrupted sleep, preferably in that order.

"Singer." The woman who'd suddenly appeared at my side barely came up to my shoulder. "If you'd come with me, I can make you a lot more comfortable in a jiffy."

Apparently, I didn't need to find my local contact—she'd found me. The woman who had magically appeared at my side was tiny, ancient, and spoke with a voice like a cannon. She was also a KarmaCorp legend. "You must be Tameka Boon." I studied her hands, encrusted with dirt, and her merry laughing eyes. "You're not what I expected."

Her lips twitched with amusement. "Good. I'd hate to be getting predictable in my old age."

My eyes were drawn back to her dirt-stained fingers —I'd seen those on Tee far too often to mistake them for anything else. "I didn't know you were a Grower too." It was highly unusual for Fixers to have more than one Talent.

Her laugh was as loud as the rest of her. "Not even kind of, child. I was a damn fine Dancer once, and occasionally my creaky hips still demand a twirl or two. But here on BroThree, you either grow your own food or you eat soy by the bucketful."

I scowled. "Soy screws with my vocal chords."

"I wasn't born yesterday." Tameka was quick-marching me down the oversized walkways that funneled space traffic through climate-controlled tubes out into the ecoverse of Bromelain III. "I've got you a full supply of Singer-approved meal packs, and your roommate was kind enough to provide me a list of some of your favorite recipes in case you'd rather eat the real thing."

I felt my eyebrows fly up into my hairline. "You cook? And you talked to Tee?" Apparently, I wasn't the only one who conducted my research through unorthodox channels.

"A lovely young lady." My host turned abruptly left. "Here, we can sneak out this way and avoid most of the lines."

Those lines were the dreaded torture otherwise known as interplanetary customs. Even in tiny space-ports, they were living hell. "Don't we have to clear the wardens first?"

She grinned. "You're awfully law abiding for a Singer."

I'd heard tales about Tameka's generation of Fixers. "You guys messed it up for the rest of us—there are a lot more rules now."

That seemed to amuse her more than anything I'd said so far. "We didn't have Yesenia regularly kicking our balls in. I hear she rides you guys pretty hard."

I knew better than to complain about the boss. "She runs a tight ship, but she's always been fair."

My host nodded, and I imagined I saw approval in her eyes. "I've heard that, too."

"Get a lot of Fixer traffic way out here?" She seemed awfully knowledgeable about how to feed, soothe, and kidnap us.

Tameka ducked through the silky folds of an egress

tunnel and beckoned me to follow. "More than you might think."

That wasn't something my mission briefing had noted. "Recent activity?"

She snorted. "You know the rules, Singer. I feed you, give you a basic orientation so you don't commit any big cultural fuck-ups during your stay here, and then I stand back and let you gather your own impressions."

She was impossible not to like. "You're awfully law abiding for a retired old fart."

Her laugh carried all the way to the end of the tunnel and bounced back at us. "Yesenia didn't send me a tame one this time." She looked up at me as she put her hand on the egress door. "Good. You'll need those sharp edges, I think."

That didn't bode well.

Then the door opened and I stopped worrying about what might happen tomorrow. A vista of undulating greens and yellows stretched as far as the eye could see. Notes rose in my throat, worshipful and unbidden.

Tameka was watching me again with those keen eyes. "This view's better than the one out the front doors of the space terminal."

It was staggering. "I've never seen anything like it— are those your grasslands?"

"The very edges of them."

The landscape moved like an ocean in slow motion, twisting in a mesmerizing dance as winds caressed grasses and the grasses rose up to meet them. I wanted to touch. Heck, I wanted to run into the vast expanse and play a cosmic game of hide-and-seek with the wind.

Tameka smiled, and I felt like I'd passed some kind of important test. "Now you know why a retired old fart like me lives here." She lifted her hand and waved at a hovering bubblepod. "Here's our ride."

I was pretty sure my ride was just getting started. "You have enough solar to power private vehicles?" By my standards, that made Bromelain III a pretty rich planet.

"Lots of sun here. And wind." Tameka ran her palm over the lock and clambered inside a lot more spryly than I managed after four days of tin canning. "And my little piece of the planet has a lovely underground spring, so we've got some micro-hydro hooked up too—that's how we power Nijinsky here."

I blinked. "Your b-pod has a name?"

"Certainly."

Curiosity gets me, every damn last time. "And who or what was Nijinsky?"

"The greatest dancer who ever lived. He loved to defy gravity." Tameka waved her hand at the dashboard. "Do you trust an old fart to drive, or would you rather I went on auto?"

I would far rather be flown by an old woman than by a pseudo-sentient glass bubble. "I'm fine with manual—I grew up on a mining asteroid."

"Ah."

A whole lot of understanding in one syllable—too much, maybe. "Ever been on a digger rock?"

"A few times." She adjusted settings on the dash and lifted Nijinsky off the ground smoothly. "It struck me as a hard life with a lot of knocks and not enough joy."

There had been some. I stared out at the vista below, trying not to think too much about a past where I'd never quite known whether I was running from or toward, and let the grasses do their hypnotic work on my tired eyes.

I woke up when Tameka banked hard right and sent my head to wobbling. The view hadn't changed much, but I had no idea how long I'd been out. "Sorry—I don't usually fall asleep on the job."

"You wouldn't be the first visitor the grasses have put to sleep."

"I hope most of them aren't driving."

She chuckled, and then banked again, less steeply this time, and glanced over at me curiously. "How'd KarmaCorp find you?"

Apparently a nap hadn't put the personal conversation to rest. "Accident. A small trader ship was out on patrol, had a Singer on board. They got lost and ran into the side of the rock I lived on."

Tameka winced, as did pretty much everyone who heard that chunk of my history. "I assume the Singer survived."

For a while. Not everyone else had been so lucky. "My dad and I were out running a survey and picked up the SOS call. When we got there, the Singer was trying to hold the trader vessel together long enough to get everyone out." The memory of her single pure, clear note ringing out into the galaxy still brought me to the edge of tears.

"Amelie Descol," said Tameka, voice reverent and sad. "I heard the story. I didn't know she'd also found a trainee."

Sending that message to KarmaCorp had been her last act before she died. They'd come for me a couple of months later, one ratty brat from a mining rock who had no idea why she heard music inside her head—or why she'd needed, every night for two months, to walk out under the dark sky and sing Amelie's note up to the stars. "Someone would have found me eventually." Karma-Corp's Seekers rarely missed.

"Likely." Her eyes scanned the horizon. "Were you happy to be found?"

"No." I wasn't sure why I'd answered—this had somehow become an uncomfortably deep foray into the personal. I could still feel the wordless fury of the fiery demon child who had discovered that her new destiny had even less flexibility than her first—and far fewer dark tunnels to hide in.

"You seem to have adjusted."

There was a clear note of sympathy in her voice, and I didn't want it. "Not much future on a mining rock." I'd learned to deal with the change from one kind of flotsam to another. And eventually, I'd found my dark tunnels, my little tastes of freedom. "It worked out okay. Things like your grasslands are a pretty nice payoff."

"Indeed."

It felt like something important had just happened,

but I had no idea what, and I was done falling asleep on the job. "You have local briefing notes for me?"

"Something like that." My host cleared her throat and sipped from a water pack. "The short version of culture, whatever that may be, here on Bromelain III. Don't stand on protocol overmuch, don't assume we're dumb farmers, and don't mess with anyone's water supplies. Manage all that, and you'll be fine."

That was as short a list as I'd ever gotten. "Sounds like a pretty tolerant place."

"People are spread out here. We keep to ourselves unless we choose company. It helps to keep the peace."

That was going to throw a few wrinkles in my mission. I needed to observe my targets, and that was a lot easier to do in a crowd. "Do you know why I'm here?"

She snorted. "Half the planet knows why you're here. Emelio Lovatt sent for you. That kind of stuff doesn't stay quiet."

I cursed Yesenia inventively in my head—her briefing had lacked that rather salient detail. "Why the heck would an Inheritor do that?" Most ruling families were very loath to give up any of their power, especially to the KarmaCorp behemoth. And no one got to send for a Fixer, not even planetary royalty. Perhaps *especially* planetary royalty. We weren't at the beck and call of people with power—we helped them when we chose.

Apparently, we had chosen.

Tameka dropped altitude and smiled mysteriously. "The Lovatts are not your typical Inheritors."

I was getting that much loud and clear. "Care to fill me in any more than that?" Generally Fixers were left to do their own investigating, and I preferred it that way, but it was pretty clear that Tameka wasn't our typical local contact.

"I think I'll leave it at that." She swung the b-pod out in a low curve, bringing us down tight over the sweeping grasslands. "We're almost at my place—you'll be staying with me tonight, and then the Lovatts are expecting you tomorrow. Their accommodations will be far plusher than mine."

I stared at her, certain I'd developed a sudden and catastrophic hearing problem. "Excuse me?"

Tameka chuckled. "Yesenia held her cards close to her chest on this one, did she?"

"That can't work." Fixers worked from the sidelines. Sometimes I went in incognito, sometimes just with a very low profile—but always, the goal was to move freely in the shadows. Staying at a freaking Inheritor's residence was anything but low profile, especially if they were the ones who had called me in.

"It will let you observe Devan Lovatt closely," said my host wryly.

It was going to put me in a bloody fishbowl. "And I suppose Janelle Brooker lives next door and comes over every night for dinner."

"Well, not every night." Tameka looked over at me, eyes glinting merrily. "And neighbors here live a little farther apart than you might be used to." She pointed a finger out my side of the bubble. "That's my shack right there. The nearest folks would be the Rideaus, and they live over that ridge."

I wasn't following her finger anymore. I was looking at the tiny, gorgeously angular building of sim-wood and glass dropped in the middle of grassland stretching as far as the eye could see. "That's yours?"

I could almost feel my host's hum of warm pleasure. "It is. It doesn't suit most."

It was my idea of paradise—full of attitude, bathed in sunshine, and really well hidden. "I don't suppose we can tell the Lovatts that I fell out the back of the cubesat and will be arriving next week instead?"

"The Inheritor will already know of your arrival." Tameka descended sharply toward her enchanting home in the middle of the high grass. "But you'd be welcome to stay at the end of your assignment, Singer. I do believe I've taken a liking to you."

I'd already figured that out—her hands were moving in the same dance Iggy's did when she greeted a friend. But it was good to hear the words anyhow. Fixers learned to take pleasurable moments when they could.

Especially at the beginning of assignments that reeked of impending disaster.

8

I SLID out the door of Tameka's tiny cabin, even in my exhaustion unable to resist the call of the glories overhead. All the glass had made it impossible to miss the blues and greens dancing cold fire across the night sky, casting weird and beautiful shadows onto the rippling gray grasslands below.

Sky magic, my father's people called it. A Dancer's heart would flourish here.

I looked around for my host, not wanting to intrude on her privacy. No one built a shack in the middle of nowhere unless they liked a whole lot of time to themselves.

"Behind you," she said, coming around the north corner of her home. "View's better from the other side, and I've got a couple bottles of cider chilling, if you like. Real stuff—I've got a friend who retired to Gaia V and sings to his apple orchards all day long. His first cider tasted like rocket fuel, but these last bottles are fairly tolerable."

I smiled—I'd been to Gaia V. Elegant, miniscule farms piled one on top of the other. They provided luxury food items to half the quadrant. The cider would be seriously prime. "You'd be claustrophobic there."

She looked out at her grasslands and laughed. "I would indeed."

I followed her around a corner, still not sure how angles and glass felt so homey. It was a far cry from the underground oval pods of my home asteroid.

The far side of Tameka's house had a small deck and two lounging chairs turned to face some hills in the distant north. The planet's twin moons hung low on the horizon, picking up blue and green shadows from the sky auroras.

I slung my butt in a chair, not at all sure I wanted to be sitting yet. It felt good enough, so I stayed.

Tameka took a seat beside me and fished around in a bucket at the side of her chair. "So what kind of name is Lakisha Drinkwater?"

Apparently, the strange personal interrogation wasn't over yet, but I was in a good enough mood to answer. "It's the kind of name you get when your mom's got Jamaican blood and your dad's sixth-generation space Cheyenne."

Her cider bottle stopped halfway to anywhere useful. "You haven't exactly got the coloring for that mix of bloodlines."

That was putting it politely. I was pale blonde Scandinavian, through and through. But whoever might have given birth to me, it was a couple of miners who had brought me to the only home my child self remembered. "My adoptive parents found me in an evac pod on the side of a crater." With a woman dead in the junker ship wreckage beside me, one of the unregistereds that collected space scrap to sell for barely enough to fuel their vessels. Ship systems, barely functional even before the crash, had routed all remaining oxygen to the evac pod and the week-old baby inside it. The Federation had been duly informed, but there were no living relatives, no one to claim me. It was a common enough story in the farther reaches of the galaxy. So I'd gone from space-junker brat to mining-rock brat.

"I'm sorry," said Tameka quietly. "It was well done of them to take you in."

I shrugged. "They were miners, and another pair of hands was always useful." I said it without rancor—they'd been decent enough parents, they just hadn't had any idea what to do with their blonde wild child.

She inclined her head in the dark. "Destiny has tossed you around some."

It had—and the two most pivotal events in my life had come when someone had crashed a tin can into a rock. I was damn glad my butt was no longer sitting in one. "I grow where I'm planted." Or I'd learned to, anyhow. With a lot of very patient help.

"Good." Tameka was back to drinking her cider. "We respect hard-won roots out here."

The colony planets usually did. It hadn't been any different back on the mining asteroid—we'd assumed that anyone who'd grown up on one of the pampered inner planets was soft. I'd met enough of those people since to have changed my impressions somewhat, but they definitely hardened up a little differently.

The show in the sky was getting more serene, but no less enthralling. "Does it do this often?"

"An hour or two most nights."

Score one for the boondocks. A quick yellow light flashed to the far left of my view. "Meteorite?"

"Nope. Visitor." My host squinted at the night sky. "Coming from the direction of the Lovatts'."

She didn't sound surprised. "Do they usually just hop on over for a visit?"

"Often enough." She smiled. "The Inheritor appreciates a good cider."

I tried to imagine a ruler of one of the inner planets dropping by for a bottle of homebrew—or Yesenia, for that matter. They'd likely give someone heart failure.

"I don't think this is Emelio, however." Tameka was still watching the light trail approaching from the west. "He drives like a man with a lot of responsibility. This must be Evgenia."

The GooglePlex had known very little other than that she existed. "Got a quick download on her?"

The retired Fixer chuckled. "I've been here going on twenty-five years now, and I don't even begin to pretend I've got Evgenia figured out. She's part farmer's daughter, part voodoo priestess, part Scottish laird."

I wasn't even sure what all those things were. "Sounds complicated."

"She is." A big pause as we both watched the incoming vehicle. "She's smart and fierce, and she loves her son dearly. And she's happiest when she's on a battlefront."

That was a whole heap more intel than I'd expected to get—and not at all reassuring. I took a cue from my host and stayed in my chair, watching as the b-pod landed with a flourish on a small circle of shorn grass and the lights flickered out.

Moments later, a woman the size of a small mountain climbed out and called over to the patio. "Evening, Tameka. I hear you have company."

"You heard right." Tameka fished again in the bucket beside her chair and made no move to get up. "Can I offer you a cider?"

"Is this the local stuff, or your special supply?"

My host chuckled. "You'll have to drink to find out."

The woman had reached our little deck, and I decided that however informal Tameka might consider the visit, I didn't want to meet this encounter lying down. I levered myself out of the lounging chair and held out a hand. "I'm Kish Drinkwater, Singer. Nice to meet you."

"Evgenia Lovatt, first and only wife of the Inheritor, if the man knows what's good for him."

I suspected that if he didn't, she'd make ship's grease out of him. "I've heard he's a smart man."

She snorted and took the bottle of cider Tameka held out. "I was hoping you'd be smart enough to ignore his request and stay home."

I hadn't been aware he'd made one until I arrived, but I wasn't about to say so. "Fixers go where we're sent."

"Just a cog in a wheel, are you?" She eyed me with an air of vague disdain. "I told Emelio we could make this happen without interference from some wisp of a girl who doesn't know a scythe from a winnower."

That was the kind of crap I couldn't take lying down, even if I didn't have the foggiest idea what a winnower was. "I'm a wisp of a girl who could spend the next ten seconds convincing you to strip naked and poop golden eggs." Or I could if KarmaCorp's ethics weren't quite so pesky.

Tameka nearly choked on her cider.

Evgenia just raised an eyebrow. "Got some spunk in there, do you?"

"My mother had some other names for it."

That almost got a smile. "I imagine."

I was exhausted, but not enough to miss the data she was sending me. She might not like my presence here, but it didn't sound like she objected to my mission's endpoint. Which might well mean she had caused its necessity—I imagined that her son was well-squished under his mother's thumb, but maybe Janelle Brooker didn't like getting pushed around.

Smart women had dug in their feet with far less cause.

My job might well be to get Evgenia out of the way. I took a sip of my cider and carefully bounced a subsonic pitch at the immense woman who was currently sizing me up. When the resonances returned, even my Talent had the sense to wince. The lowest base note I'd ever heard, and rock solid to boot.

Evgenia would be about as easy to influence as an intergalactic battle cruiser. Doable, but painful as hell. I watched as she turned to make small talk with my host and hoped like heck it wouldn't come to that.

9

IN AN ACT of morning obstinance that my mother would have recognized well, I'd decided to go meet Janelle Brooker first, rather than do the politically prudent thing and introduce myself to the Lovatts' doormat of a son.

That bit of fun could wait for later.

I rolled Tameka's bubblepod in a sweet lefthand bank, happy as sin to be driving. Most Fixers could barely manage the basics of flying a private vehicle, but I'd grown up on a digger rock, and a pilot's daughter to boot. I'd handled our old and jangly b-pod before I'd lost my front teeth. I took one last three-sixty for fun and because I could, and then headed toward the sprawling angles of the building that, according to my host's directions, housed the woman who'd so far managed to evade the wishes of both the man who ran her planet and his gladiator wife.

Three or four people looked up and waved in friendly fashion, and all of them seemed to be pointing me toward a stand of trees left of the house. I spied a landing circle just past the trees and dropped the hover feet. The b-pod floated into an effortless landing that would hopefully impress the natives and keep Tameka from revoking my flying privileges. It had taken some fast talking and a quick demo to get her to lend me Nijinsky at all.

By the time I'd put the b-pod into stationary, a young woman had made her way over to the edge of the landing circle. She watched me steadily as I climbed out and planted my feet on the ground. I waved what I hoped looked like a friendly hello. She had lots of reasons not to like me. "Good morning—you must be Janelle Brooker."

"Am." She smiled. "And you must be Lakisha Drinkwater, the quadrant's most talked-about Singer at the ripe old age of twenty-five."

Apparently, the GooglePlex had been forthcoming—and full of the usual lies and half-truths. "People need more to talk about. And everyone calls me Kish."

She smiled again. "I'm guessing most call you Singer, but Kish will do just fine." She held up her hand, two red fruits on her palm. "Ever had an apple?"

My mouth was already watering. "I have, but it's an experience I'm really happy to repeat." Assuming it wasn't poisoned—I knew my fairy tales well enough, and it was positively weird that Janelle was being so friendly. "Why are you being so nice?"

Her laugh was friendly and open, and teased at my

Talent as she tossed an apple my way. "I'm nice to most people. We've got a whole orchard of apples that are ripe and ready, so help yourself any time you like."

Generosity was obviously a way of life here. I tried to respond in kind as best as I could. "My roommate back on Stardust Prime likes to bake pies."

Janelle's eyes lit up. "Any chance you could get a recipe? Dad's got plenty of good ones to trade."

Recipes were often better galactic currency than money—and if pie instructions would buy me some Brooker goodwill, I'd deliver them by the tablet full. "I'd be happy to hook the two of them up."

"It'll have to be in a few days. My parents are on Andromethius visiting my brother and my new baby niece. I'm holding down the fort."

Andromethius was an outpost colony on the other side of the quadrant. I debated, and then raised an eyebrow at the woman walking under the trees beside me. "That sounds like pretty convenient timing."

She offered a small smile up at a tree. "I wondered if you'd pick that up."

It wasn't the only thing I was picking up. My Talent was in gear and collecting first impressions—and underneath Janelle's bright and friendly exterior rode some serious steel. I'd found at least some of the spine I'd been sent to bend. "I would imagine the Inheritor invited me here at a time when he thought my work would be most likely to succeed." Even strong people wither faster in isolation.

Her shoulders hitched upward a fraction. "Emelio

Lovatt is a smart man."

There was a really loud thought she wasn't saying. "But?"

Janelle chuckled and took a bite of her apple. "But he doesn't understand family nearly as well as he thinks he does."

I contemplated that for a while as I made sure not a drop of the sharp and sweet apple juice missed my mouth. "His family isn't exactly typical."

She raised a quirky eyebrow and grinned. "I take it you've met Evgenia."

To put it mildly. "She flew into Tameka's place last evening for a visit."

A second eyebrow quirk. "Interesting."

That word could mean a thousand different things.

Janelle hesitated a moment. "Don't underestimate her. She's more than just her bluster—some of her best moves are the ones she makes quietly while everyone's watching the dust of whatever drama she's just created."

That was also interesting, especially considering the source—and not a vibe I'd picked up from my first short encounter with Evgenia. "Not as straightforward as she appears?"

"She's married to an Inheritor."

That could make her anything from arm decoration to the power behind the throne. "Does she wear the pants in the family?"

Janelle nearly choked on her apple. "I take it you haven't met Emelio yet."

I was going to stuff the KarmaCorp briefing file up

Yesenia's compost valve when I got back to Stardust Prime. "I take it he's interesting too."

She made a wry face. "Very. They're a hell of a couple."

I wasn't at all sure of Janelle's motives at the moment, but I appreciated the data. "They're a couple who want you married to their only son."

She took a bite of her apple. "Yes."

The friendly vibe was still there—but it walked beside a wary one. "I assume you try to stay out of their way?"

"No."

In that one word, I finally saw on the surface what my Talent had sensed underneath. Steel, and not so hidden anymore. I raised an eyebrow of my own. "Why not?" I looked around at the sweeping grasslands that bordered the apple orchard. "It's a big planet."

"It is." Janelle gazed out at the horizon for a while, a woman entirely comfortable with what was hers. "But I don't ever intend to give those two the impression I might be herdable."

My own Song resonated, loudly. If my mission had been collecting friends on backwater planets, I'd be set. Instead, I'd been sent to bend the will of this smart, articulate, independent woman to what the StarReaders had decided was her appropriate destiny.

Which I wasn't exactly feeling inclined to do. She'd fed me an apple, dammit.

She glanced over at me. "I assume you got sent to see

if I could be persuaded to drop my knickers and hop into Devan's lap."

I nearly snorted apple juice out my nose. BroThree didn't grow people who beat around the bush. Fortunately, neither did digger rocks. "Yeah, I was."

She was looking at me straight on now. "Could you do it?"

That was one of those questions we weren't supposed to answer. "Yeah." I shrugged. "I could get you in his lap, anyhow. The knicker dropping would be up to you." KarmaCorp had their ethical lines, and I had mine, and at least in Yesenia's corner of the galaxy, the two were pretty much in agreement.

"Good to know."

One kind of honesty deserved another. "Is there a reason you aren't already in his lap?"

Her chuckle was melodic, light, and wry. "You mean besides my general objection to being a cog in someone else's plans?"

I winced. Fixers were often accused of being cog greasers, and our accusers weren't wrong. "Yeah, besides that." I needed the more personal objections, whatever they were. "Is he ugly, obnoxious, weak, short?"

"No." She smiled. "Devan's not any of those things."

I was surprised at the clear affection in her tone and in her eyes. "You like him."

"I do." Janelle was back to watching her grasslands, voice flat and calm. "But I don't love him in any kind of romantic sense, I don't imagine that will change, and I'm not some feudal princess who can be ordered to marry a guy to save the empire."

There were worlds like that in the Federation, ones that pampered their royals thoroughly and gave them very little in the way of choices. That seemed at deep odds with what I saw when I looked out at the grasslands, though. This planet had been shaped by souls who knew freedom well.

She shrugged and tossed her apple core into a patch of curly fronds. "Besides, I'm in no hurry to pair up with anyone. I have a good life and a busy one, and from what I can gather, men are a lot of work."

Amen to that. Her words rang true with my Talent, too—it wasn't Devan in particular she objected to, but the plan to marry her off in general. Which raised an obvious question that I still didn't have a satisfactory answer to. It was time to figure out more of why I'd really been sent to BroThree. "So there's one thing I'm not at all clear on."

She glanced at me, amused. "Only one?"

Smart and funny. "For the moment. Why are some people so determined that the two of you get hitched?" It was the politest way I could think of to ask why Karma-Corp was sticking their nose into the internal politics of some backwater planet. She wouldn't know all the answers—but she likely knew more than I did.

She snorted. "You should ask them."

I intended to. "You're smart, you have your eyes open, and you've lived here your whole life. I've been here sixteen hours. Help me out."

"Only if you promise not to mess with my knickers."

That much I could promise—and only that much. "Done."

"How much do you know about colony planets?"

Enough to know they all had a different story. "Assume I'm a dumb flatlander from one of the inner worlds."

She grinned. "They don't call themselves dumb flatlanders."

Not usually. "I grew up on a digger rock."

"Huh." Her head tilted to the side, thinking. "I don't know much about mining asteroids—how do they get started?"

A lot more simply than most colonies. "Some poor schmucks get shipped to a cold rock with a bunch of digging tools. The ones who figure out how to use the tools fastest usually end up in charge. If you're lucky, they're good people."

"Was your rock lucky?" Janelle stuck her hands in her pockets, voice carefully casual.

I wondered what she'd heard. "Close enough."

"Good." She nodded, back to watching her grasslands. It seemed like a fairly major occupation here. "It's not all that different on a colony planet. A few extended families get shipped in to get things started."

That much they taught even in digger grade school. "The Founders." Seeds of a new society.

"Yeah." She shrugged. "If you're lucky, they're good people."

Ah. "Things got sticky here?"

"A nasty virus cropped up, killed a quarter of the colonists before the medicals found a cure." Her lips pursed. "And a couple of families on the rampage killed another quarter before they got stopped."

The fear of imminent death on a lonely rock didn't bring out the best in everyone. "What happened?"

"My grandfather led the colonists who stopped the rampage. He was also the guy who found the cure—he was just a tech, but the virus had wiped out most of the medical team."

That was the kind of thing that would inspire some pretty solid loyalty. "Interesting blood running in your veins." She hadn't been picked at random for this marriage deal.

She smiled wryly. "It gets more interesting. My grandfather convinced my grandmother to run off with him to settle here. Her father was Jackson Douglas's youngest brother."

The Saskatchewan farming clan that had explored and mapped half the quadrant. Galactic royalty, and another reason the power structure on this planet was a lot less straightforward than it seemed. I looked over at Janelle, feeling my way through the shifting melody line of the words she'd said, and the ones she hadn't. "So who really runs this place?" Inheritors were supposed to rule their planets—but I was looking at the bright, ambitious, driven granddaughter of the man who had pulled BroThree out of self-destruct.

Janelle smiled and shrugged. "That depends a lot on

who you ask. The Lovatts have the ear of the Federation Council."

Galactic royalty had thumbed their noses at local rulers before, and at the Commonwealth Council for that matter. Competing seats of power were inherently messy and could send ripples far out into the galaxy. That was the kind of reason that could easily mobilize KarmaCorp troops. This mission wasn't about a marriage—it was about a merger. "So people figure you and Devan marrying each other stabilizes things here."

She made a face. "Do things seem unstable to you?"

They didn't, but I'd only been here sixteen hours. And KarmaCorp often targeted latent instability—ripples that hadn't happened yet. "If it would help your planet, would you marry him?" That was walking awfully close to unbendable lines with an Ears Only file, but I needed to know what levers I had to work with. What mattered to Janelle Brooker.

She was watching me carefully. "You're very good at your job, aren't you?"

I was, but I didn't think she was handing me a compliment. "I'm just saying that there might be more than your personal happiness at stake." And colonists were carefully selected to put the greater good first, even on a planet that seemed as freedom bound as this one.

"There might be." She shrugged. "There often is. But I can only go with what I know, and right now, nobody's making a convincing case for changing my mind."

I could hear her steadiness. Her solid trust in her own skills and her own choices, her belief that her destiny was her own to drive. I closed my eyes and sighed. Given the right data, Janelle Brooker would probably do what it was that StarReaders wanted. And for reasons only they knew—they'd decided not to provide it.

They'd sent me to do their dirty work instead.

10

AFTER TAMEKA'S tiny cabin and the Brookers' comfortable, sprawling ranch, I'd somehow expected the Lovatts to live in something resembling an actual house.

I couldn't have been more wrong. The Lovatt compound was something out of an old-school fantasy novel, complete with turrets, stone walls, and the kinds of weapons sticking out windows that were banned by at least a dozen kinds of Federation law.

"They're none of them armed," said a smiling woman passing by, her arms full of linens. "At least that's what the Inheritor tells anyone who comes to inspect them."

I watched her go, clad in a dress that looked like it came from the same era as the weapons.

"Someone will be here to greet you in a moment." The guard who had waylaid me at the gate was most decidedly from this century, as was the blaster at his hip.

I decided to see how good security was. "This place

looks like three vid sets got sucked up by a tornado and spit back out."

He managed not to laugh, but just barely. "The Inheritor's residence never fails to impress guests."

I bet.

"Singer." A young man with a slight build and quick eyes had materialized at my left shoulder. "If you'll come this way, your presence is requested in the Rose courtyard."

Roses had thorns. First message delivered, by whoever had sent it. I had my suspicions.

"Are you sure, Jordi?" The guard raised a quiet eyebrow that managed to communicate uncertainty and calm reassurance at the same time.

"Quite sure." The slender man spared an extra glance at the guard before gesturing toward a left-curving path.

I sent out a quiet ping as I fell in behind him—he moved gracefully enough that I wouldn't have been surprised to discover he was a Dancer. Nothing came back. Just a guy with some fluid moves on a backwater planet, walking me to my doom.

I grinned—apparently the gothic ambience was catching me up in its web, but I was nobody's prey. I was a Singer here to gauge the lay of the land and get a closer look at the other half of the Brooker-Lovatt merger.

"Singer."

The path had abruptly ended in a courtyard straight out of a creepy fairy tale. Roses climbed tall walls, creating the instant impression of a very fragrant prison. I studied the woman seated on a dais in the center. She certainly knew how to make an impression. "Hello again, Evgenia."

She glanced around the thorny cage she'd fetched me to. "You'll be shown to your rooms in a moment, and I trust they will be comfortable. I wanted to speak with you first."

There were undertones to what she was saying, but they were muddy and unclear. I did what I should have done at the front gates and let my Talent unfurl a little. Passive mode only, but it would help me catch the nuances. "I'm happy to listen."

"I want you to do more than that." Her tone was clipped, quick, and final—the words of a woman used to having her commands followed. "You're about to enjoy the legendary hospitality of the Lovatts. In exchange, I expect the courtesy of being informed before you take any actions that might unduly affect members of my household."

That was blunt—and impossible. "I'm afraid I can't do that. My freedom to act as I see fit is enshrined in Council covenant." The Warriors of Karma had been very thorough.

She raised an eyebrow. "I didn't ask to control your actions—only to be notified of them in advance."

A questionable distinction, and a meaningless one. "You didn't *ask*."

My Talent buzzed an unnecessary alert—Evgenia's

temper was easy enough to read on her face. "This is my home, Singer, and you'd do well to remember that."

My own temper snapped. *Enough.* I sang a sharp staccato trio, this time letting the notes be clearly audible. A warning—and a bit of a threat. No one leaned on a Singer, not unless she was under orders to let it happen.

Evgenia's eyes clouded with disdain, even as they widened a little. "I'd have thought you were above that sort of parlor trick."

I'd been accused of worse. "It's only a parlor trick if I can't deliver."

That got rid of some of the disdain. "I don't like you, Singer."

Oddly enough, that wasn't ringing true in my harmonics. "So long as you respect my Talent and my right to be here, that will be enough." It wouldn't be—I didn't like getting kicked at any more than the next person, and I fully intended to hold a grudge—but it was the kind of politic answer that a representative of Karma-Corp was expected to give.

She snorted, but a decent amount of the wind had gone out of her sails. "Stick with threats. You're a damn poor liar."

I wasn't here to be one. "Fortunately, I'm a much better Singer."

"We shall see." Evgenia stared down her nose at me. "However, whatever else Yesenia may have sent us, I don't think you're a pushover."

It was good we'd gotten that much straight.

"Ah, here you are."

I turned to watch the arrival of the person who belonged to the smooth and powerful voice. He moved out of the shadows of the entry portico, a tall man with dark hair, dark eyes, and the stride of someone who knew he walked on lands he ruled.

He was also a man with excellent timing. I held out my hands, palms up, and slid into full diplomatic mode. "Greetings, Inheritor. I deeply appreciate the hospitality of you and your family while I'm here."

He smiled and cast his wife a long glance. "I trust it won't involve too many more detours before we've managed to get you a bed and a decent meal or two."

I was very glad I wasn't standing any closer to Evgenia—her eyes looked ready to light things on fire. "We were just talking about Director Mayes, Inheritor. She sends you her best wishes, and those of KarmaCorp as well."

The Inheritor chuckled. "She did no such thing. And I would be pleased to have you call me Emelio, as every citizen of this planet does."

The waters of this assignment just kept getting murkier. I needed to change that, and if Evgenia and her thorns were any indication, I needed to do it pretty damn fast. I took a steadying breath. "Thank you, Emelio. I appreciate the warm welcome, and I'm glad to have a chance to speak with you about why I've been sent here." The reasons on his radar, anyhow.

"To a lowly colony planet, you mean?" Evgenia's eyes were sharp, her voice sharper. "Don't underestimate the citizens of Bromelain III, Singer. We'll be eligible for

Federated status in three more years, and I intend to see that we get it."

She fired a last seething glance at her husband and moved off in a storm of stomp and fury, immediately pulling a young woman in uniform garb into animated discussion. All while staying close enough to hear exactly what was said next.

I pondered, and looked at the man standing beside me. Federation membership was the Holy Grail for colony planets, and it wasn't handed out lightly. "Will you get status?"

He tilted his head slightly and smiled. "Evgenia will be on the warpath if we don't."

I raised an eyebrow. Strong men didn't usually hide behind their wife's skirts, even as a conversational gambit. "And you?"

"I will abide by the Council's decision." His face gave nothing away.

Fortunately, I had better sensors—and my Talent said he wanted membership in the Commonwealth at least as much as his wife. Which explained why they'd asked for me. The Council liked new member planets to be neat and tidy, and a marriage of the colony's two most powerful families would tidy this one up considerably.

That's why I'd been requested. However, I doubted it was actually the reason I'd been sent. StarReaders didn't get involved over the fate of a backwater planet, not unless it sent some serious ripples elsewhere.

Ripples I didn't need to understand, at least not today. I was tired, annoyed, and I wasn't here to practice my diplomatic waltzing, a class I'd barely passed as a trainee in the first place. Some Fixers navigated the political waters of their assignments with ease, but I wasn't one of them. In the immortal words of one of my instructors, I tended to work like a kid who had grown up on the business end of a drill bit. Success had earned me some politer descriptors, but I still tended to be sent on missions where it was decently likely I would need to throw a punch.

Hopefully, that wasn't going to happen on this one—Emelio's nose looked pretty hard. I studied his face as he guided us out of the rose garden and back into more populated areas, and recalled one of his wife's carefully aimed thorns—the one where she had called my boss by her first name. "How do you know Director Mayes, Inheritor?"

His eyes got careful and distant. "I met her when she worked in the field."

I blinked—Yesenia had been a Traveler. As far as I knew, none of her assignments would have been in the current timeline.

Emelio waved at someone off in the distance. "And no, I won't answer any further questions about that. Neither, I imagine, will she."

Yesenia didn't tend to answer questions, period. "Fair enough. How about a new question, then—why am I here to help two grown adults fall in love?"

He didn't move, but his face sharpened with interest. "Why don't you tell me how much of the answer you've already worked out?"

That was neatly done, but I imagined he was a pro at ducking questions he didn't want to answer. "You've got a planet with two families that could call the shots. I don't know yet whether you coexist reasonably well, but I imagine that worries the Federation bureaucrats."

That earned me my first unscripted smile. "You've been busy."

"Just doing my job." I was pretty sure that if he'd wanted that information buried, it would have been a lot harder to find. Then again, so far BroThree hadn't struck me as a place where anyone was used to being muzzled. "So, do you and the Brookers play nicely together in the sandbox or not?"

He raised one shoulder in a classically Gallic shrug. "Any society with two ruling powers is inherently unstable."

That was a central tenet of the political theory that had given rise to the Inheritor model. One decently capable boss, less planetary strife. "So you're going to solve the problem by merger?" Not a totally dumb idea— it happened a lot in the old-school fantasy novels I drank like water.

A chuckle again. "Nothing nearly so businesslike, my dear. I'm a romantic at heart. I hope my son finds true love."

It came off as a throwaway line, but my Talent heard the quiet harmonics of truth underneath. Emelio Lovatt was ambitious, canny, concerned about his wife's machinations—and he wanted his only son to be happy.

That was why he had asked for a Fixer. He wanted

his son to walk willing, or even eager, into a marriage that would keep the natives content, the Federation appeased, and his wife off the battlefield. My job was to smooth the way and nudge the two dominos that would tip the rest into place.

I hid a grin. Janelle would not appreciate any part of being compared to a domino. Which, even if it made my job significantly harder, I had to respect.

It was a good thing I liked improvising—this mission had already blown the usual operating manual all to hell. But at least I was beginning to assemble information.

What I needed to know next was how Devan fit into this picture. With two powerhouse parents, I assumed he was either a browbeaten son who said yes to everything or a dilettante who had abandoned responsibility altogether. Most rich and powerful families had a steady supply of both.

I turned toward the Inheritor, careful to keep my external demeanor impassive. "I'd like to meet your son."

He flashed me a charismatic, sexy smile. "That's what all the pretty girls say."

The man had more masks than the planet Venetia during Carnivale. He'd also managed to make sure I was well informed in less than five minutes, within earshot of his wife. And he'd convinced Yesenia to send me here in the first place. Definitely not a man to underestimate. He'd pissed me off by calling me pretty, though. "Including Janelle?"

"Janelle Brooker is a lovely young lady." He was as smooth as Tee's silk hankies. "She and Devan have been good friends for a lifetime, and I'd be most pleased at the chance to welcome her into our family."

I looked over to where Evgenia stood, regal, annoyed, and clearly listening. "And how do you feel about Janelle, Madame Inheritor?"

Her sniff was probably audible on BroThree's twin moons. "Any woman would be lucky to have my son."

In other words, she was a biased mama miffed that Janelle hadn't fallen at Devan's feet.

I wondered if it mattered to either of them what Janelle wanted. I felt my Song buzz a quiet harmonic of sisterhood, and cut it off. I wasn't here to be sympathetic. In the end, I might not be able to care that much about what Janelle Brooker wanted either.

"You've asked some very direct questions, Singer." Emelio's words were polite, his eyes reflecting only casual interest. "Perhaps you will permit me to ask one or two as well."

Not happily, but I was pretty sure that wasn't an answer he heard very often. "Certainly, although I retain the right not to answer."

The gleam in his eye said he didn't hear that very often either. "Tell me about your last assignment."

That sounded more like the beginning of a job interview than a question. "I was sent to one of the new greenhouse biomes. A small splinter group was on the edge of revolt." Which probably wouldn't have merited a Fixer's attention except the biome produced a couple of vital medical ingredients, and one of the splinter group members had been pretty handy at building things that exploded.

Emelio inclined his head like he'd heard my unspoken words as well. "And why the rebellion?"

Mostly reasons I couldn't give him. "A handful of people couldn't handle the wide-open spaces." The new greenhouse planets had them in abundance.

He nodded sagely. "Inner-planet volunteers, I take it."

He'd managed to keep the disdain from his voice, but my Talent heard it anyway. And he wasn't wrong. Seeding colonies was art, not science, and the failure rate, even with the help of the KarmaCorp Anthros, was still high enough to make Federation bureaucratic types cringe. The psychs could run all the tests they wanted, but in the end, they were only guessing—the only sure way to tell if someone from an overcrowded cage of an inner planet could handle a view of the unencumbered sky was to let them see it.

Emelio had paused in a corner of the compound that gave a convenient and impressive view over much of the grounds. "And your role was to calm the revolt?"

Something like that. "I'm good at my job, if that's what you're asking."

He smiled. "It's one of the things I'm asking."

The man could charm the scales off a fish. "You expect me to be calming a revolt here, do you?"

His laugh rang out through the compound. "You'll do, Singer. It appears Yesenia did good work in sending you."

Evgenia sniffed audibly in the background.

I had no idea why she hadn't simply joined us at this point, but it didn't matter. They might have very different opinions of me, but both Lovatts clearly supported my mission's intended outcome. Which was good news—allies didn't have to be friendly ones. "I hope I'll have the opportunity to meet your son soon, Inheritor." Whatever bigger forces were in play, my job was here on the ground.

Emelio looked past my shoulder, his eyes lighting with pleasure and welcome. "You're about to get your wish."

I assumed the Inheritor Elect was home, and gathered my Talent. Time to let Devan Lovatt make his first impression. Harmonics in place, I turned, ready to collect data.

He wasn't hard to find. Devan was the spitting image of a younger Emelio, with added hints of Evgenia's fire. Tall, wiry muscle, he moved into the rotunda with the spare grace of a space pilot and the friendly exuberance of a man who had once been a boy running these grounds.

And then he was a man on the run.

I scanned the direction he was charging and winced, seeing the impending collision just before it happened. A young boy flying across the lawn, looking back over his shoulder—and half a step away from running headlong into an older girl carrying a stack of holobooks.

I could hear the collective intake of breath as the crash happened. The girl landed in an ungraceful lump, holobooks spraying out over several meters. The boy arced through the air and plowed face-first into the grass, followed a moment later by the crash landing of a toy cubesat just past his outstretched fingers.

A frozen moment, and then ten people arrived on the scene all at once. Hands reached out to dry the girl's tears, collect up her belongings, soothe her scraped knees.

There were a few glances at the boy crawling over to cuddle his smashed toy. Enough to verify he wasn't hurt —and to communicate their collective exasperation with the reckless child who hadn't taken enough care.

My heart squeezed. I'd been him, so damn many times. I wanted, badly, to do something. To say something. To remind all those people that reckless hearts bruised too.

And then Devan Lovatt was there, scooping up a small boy and his smashed toy and settling both into his lap. A dozen people bustling, fixing, managing—and the Inheritor Elect of Bromelain III sat down on a patch of grass, hugged a small boy's head, and touched gentle fingers to the sad, dangling solar wings of a busted model cubesat.

Offering comfort. Lamenting a wounded treasure.

The scene on the lawn changed. The brusque busyness around the girl shifted and a couple of friendly faces crouched down by Devan and the boy in his lap. One offered a gentle rub on the child's knee. Another dug into her pockets and came out with a wrapped sweet and a tube of instaglue. Finding their kindness, their empathy for a small boy who didn't look before he leaped.

Following the lead of the man who would one day lead them. The man who had, in the space of a few seconds, made a very intentional choice to stand for one small boy—and to nudge those around him without ever saying a word.

I could feel my brain noting the data, tracking what my harmonics were reading, stashing the observations for later. Which was good, because the rest of me was barely managing to stay inside my skin. My hands were clammy, my forehead was hot, and my chakras had melted into an auric puddle of goo.

Or as Tee would have put it, my hormones had just lit up like a Galactic Peace Day light show.

I knew I was in big trouble. My Song was mutating into something that resembled a freaking mating call and the guy who would run this planet someday was touching a small boy's face one last time and climbing to his feet.

I swallowed once, my mouth dry as rock dust. And then I remembered that I was a Singer—someone who deserved respect and who could command it if necessary. "I'd prefer to meet with the Inheritor Elect later." The steadiness of my voice was an abject lie, but it would fool anyone not Talented.

Emelio raised an eyebrow, clearly taken aback. Evgenia's face resembled a Renusian thunderstorm.

Clear evidence that I needed to beat my retreat a whole lot more graciously. I offered up what I hoped was a rueful smile. "My apologies—I'm suddenly quite tired from the travel. I believe I'd like to spend some time in my rooms now."

I had no idea if either of them believed me, but as I followed a hastily summoned staffer out of the sunlight and into a dim hallway, I didn't much care. Hiding might not be a life strategy my mother respected much, but every kid from a digger rock knew it had its uses.

Devan Lovatt was as good a reason as I'd ever had.

11

I WASN'T sure what life forms had made the little trails I was following through the high grass, but they surely weren't human. Or headed anywhere purposeful.

No matter—the aimless wandering suited my mood. My assignment had just turned into even more of a clusterfuck, and I had no idea what to do about it.

Damn hormones.

And not just hormones. Devan Lovatt had shaken me silly, but Janelle had landed a few blows as well. A target who thought her desires and choices mattered was pretty standard on a KarmaCorp mission. Most people believed in the greater good, right up until they had to personally sacrifice for it. That's why my job was to nudge, to make sure the ripples that happened were the right ones. But this time I'd be leaning on someone I liked, and I was out here partly because that royally sucked.

"Lost?"

The single word nearly jolted me into outer orbit.

Tameka unfolded herself from her seat on the ground and stood, holding out a hand in welcome. "If you're trying to get somewhere, I can promise you this path isn't going to work."

"I was just taking a walk."

She looked me up and down. "I see."

I hoped my outer layers were distracting enough to keep her from looking any deeper. Before I fled the Lovatt compound, I'd ditched the KarmaCorp skinsuit and pulled on my mangiest pair of puff pants. They were billowy, flowy, and cool, and the wind that seemed to constantly tease the Bromelain III grasslands was having a field day with them. I stuffed my hands in their over-sized pockets and focused on the feeling of being really aware of my skin. It had soothed a blonde demon child once—maybe it would work today, too.

Tameka was watching my pants with interest. "Those don't look like digger-rock gear."

"They aren't." No miner would be caught dead in anything with loose, flowing fabric unless they had an almighty death wish. The pants were a habit I'd picked up from Tee's family, which was full of voracious gardeners and martial artists.

My host hefted a medium-sized rock and tossed it at a small pile of them on the side of the path. "So, what has you wandering aimlessly along my fence line?"

I looked around, surprised—I hadn't seen any fences.

She smiled. "Figure of speech, mostly. The bound-aries between properties are electronic in these parts. You've crossed into my lands."

"Glad I'm not on a planet that shoots first and asks questions later."

"These days, that's a reasonably safe assumption."

I was growing the sneaking suspicion that BroThree had a far less placid history than the official docs suggested. "I didn't mean to trespass—I was just looking for a little air to clear my head."

"We have lots of that available." Tameka rocked back on her heels, hands in her pockets. "What's got you on the run?"

It was entirely embarrassing to be caught at it. "I was looking for somewhere I could hear myself think." I winced at the whiny complaint in my voice. "There are a lot of people stuffed into that compound."

"You're welcome at my place any time you like."

It was a generous invitation, and a tempting one. "I have a job to do."

"Indeed." Approval tinged her words—and a hint of exasperation. "But one can't always do a job every hour of the day. If you have need of a bit of sheltering before you're done here, consider my home yours to use as you wish."

Her home was a tiny piece of galactic magic, and I had no intention of sliming it with the shit I was suddenly neck deep in. Tameka herself was a different matter, however. She was old and tough and totally capable of taking care of herself. "Do you have any idea why Emelio Lovatt has pull with Yesenia?" It wasn't the most important thing I needed to figure out, but it was a start.

My host's eyebrows flew up in surprise. "No. But the

Inheritor is a smart man. You'd do well not to underestimate him."

I'd already figured that much out. "That seems to be true of a lot of people around here."

She smiled. "You've met our lovebirds then, have you?"

I hadn't actually managed to meet the Inheritor Elect. But Janelle had been entirely impressive, and whatever else Devan Lovatt might be, he clearly wasn't the browbeaten son I'd imagined—even fleeting first impressions had incinerated that idea. "So how is it that two smart, interesting, attractive people who grew up together haven't managed to at least try the bed-buddies deal?"

Tameka raised an eyebrow. "You're sure of that, are you?"

"Yes." Talent rarely misread something that basic, and my read on Janelle had been good and solid. "Trainees hop into bed with each other all the time." It was a fairly natural occurrence when you had randy teenagers sharing the same oxygen supply. "Why not these two?"

The wind whipped my pants, picking up on my frustration—multiple flavors of it.

Tameka shrugged. "Chemistry's easy when it happens, and hell when it doesn't."

I was living proof of that at the moment. And suddenly curious—Dancers were good at sparking things. A Singer wasn't actually the obvious Talent to have sent to intervene here. "Has anyone ever given them a nudge?"

"You mean, did I come out of retirement long enough to try to steer the love lives of a couple of healthy adults?" She chuckled and tipped her head up to the sky. "No. And as far as I know, I'm the only person on Bromelain III with enough Talent to do so."

I squinted, suddenly suspicious. "Did Yesenia ask you to try?"

My host looked at me, eyes steady, but opaque. "Yes."

I felt my insides, already rattled from Janelle and Devan, dump into a blender. Fixers didn't say no— trainee tadpoles were regularly scared with stories of the few who had tried. That kind of rebellion happened very rarely, and when it did, no one got to retire happily to fields of grass. "You said no?"

Tameka was watching me carefully. "It's not the first time I've done that."

My brain stuttered to a halt. The woman in front of me was a Fixer legend. Of the good kind, not the tadpole-scaring variety.

She raised a wry eyebrow. "They're still white-washing my story in the hallowed halls of KarmaCorp, are they?"

I shuffled my feet just enough to make sure the laws of gravity were still working. I could buy that they controlled what the trainees heard, but there was no way Yesenia didn't know.

I was looking at a real-live Fixer who had said no.

More than once.

And drank apple cider on her porch.

My vaunted ability to improvise crash-landed and

skittered off into the grass. And somewhere inside me, fascination rose. The blonde, fiery demon child, curious as all hell. I tried to squish her back into the cave she'd come out of.

Tameka watched me steadily. "Ask, girl—no one's here to listen."

"Why didn't you lean on them?" It wasn't the most important question I wanted to ask, but it was the least dangerous—and the most relevant to getting my mission done.

Tameka took her hands out of her pockets and raised her arms like she was about to carry a watermelon. "I held Janelle when she was just a tiny thing. I was brand new here and heard that her mama was sick. I came by to drop off some soup, and they put this wrapped, squalling bundle in my arms to see if I could do anything to quiet her." She laughed softly. "I'd barely put my feet down on the planet, and I hadn't so much as seen a baby in sixty years. It was scarier than being handed a neutron bomb."

I had some idea—Tee had a lot of little, squalling cousins. "What did you do?"

"I Danced." Her eyes hazed over, a woman remembering. "For hours, I held her, and together we touched the first air she breathed, the first sunlight, the first winds over the grass. They were some of my first winds here too. We shared that."

Realization dawned, bright and shiny and horrifying. "You love her."

"I do." Tameka's hands were back in her pockets. "I didn't mean for you to know that just yet."

Some things you couldn't walk backwards. "You didn't mean for me to know it at all."

She shrugged. "I didn't expect to like you."

That was going to be an issue for both of us. "Are you going to try to keep me from doing my job?"

She sighed. "If I thought Janelle and Devan could be happy together, I'd be the first in line to help you push."

"You don't think they'd be happy?"

"Some people live easily with mediocrity, with settling for something that isn't exactly right." She tossed a small rock hand to hand. "But you and I, we aren't those people. Neither are Janelle and Devan."

If this hadn't already turned into a pisser of a mission, it would have gone down that drain now. "I don't want to be in a sparring match with a wily old Dancer."

"Oh, I won't get in your way." She smiled and dropped the rock in her pocket. "I won't need to."

That was about as comforting as an oxygen tank on zero. Exactly like what had chased me out here in the first place.

12

I YAWNED hard enough to crack my jaw as I padded my way into the enormous room where I'd been told that the Lovatts served breakfast. It was a huge, echoing space, stopped just shy of ostentatious by the wall of windows that showed the shimmering morning light on the grasslands.

Proof that there were riches and beauty in abundance beyond the walls of this compound.

I made my way over to the buffet table set out against one wall, my bare feet sinking deep into the carpet. Not all that different from the mud I'd run around in as a kid. My stomach hadn't ever been this well courted back then, though—whatever else I might think about my hosts, a quick glance said they knew how to feed people. Platters were laid out as far as the eye could see, loaded with solid, stomach-sticking food, and all of it real. I hadn't spied soy anything since I'd stepped off the transpo ferry. Back-water planets had some upsides.

I picked up a plate and surveyed my choices. I'd missed dinner last night out of sheer cowardice, and my appetite was fierce.

"The eggs are good."

My plate nearly embedded itself in Devan Lovatt's skull. "Dammit, do you always sneak up on people that way?"

He grinned and took a plate of his own. "Nope. Mom says I make more noise than a herd of space elephants."

Space elephants walking on four-centimeter-thick carpet, maybe. Belatedly, I realized that he might not have the foggiest clue who I was. I held up a hand in the universal galactic sign of greeting—given the jangles he'd set off all over my body, it seemed safer than touching. "Lakisha Drinkwater."

"I know who you are." Devan was already reaching out and forking things onto his plate. He dropped a slice of long, skinny meat that smelled like nirvana onto mine. "Ever tried bacon? Food of the gods, right there."

I was still feeling prickly from his sneaky arrival and the all-too-obvious effect he was having on my hormones. Parts of me were waking up way too fast. "No. Mining rocks don't tend to run to meat."

He raised an eyebrow at my tone. "Sorry. Didn't mean to bring up bad memories."

He hadn't, and I was being a first-class bitch. "No, the apology's mine. I woke up cranky and apparently I haven't fixed it yet."

He smiled. "Try the bacon. It fixes pretty much everything."

Like Janelle, he wasn't putting out any hostile vibes at all, which was entirely weird. Neither of them were acting very damn concerned about my presence. However, that was a problem I would worry about after I had consumed copious amounts of bacon. I reached for a spoon of something red and spicy and put a small pile of it in the middle of my plate. It smelled like something Raven would love.

"That's salsa—it's supposed to go on top of your eggs. Here." Devan neatly switched my plate for his very full one. "I'll give you a tour of the food after we eat some. I'm starving."

I wanted to kick him in the shins for treating me like a two-year-old, but that would just prove his point. I also knew that sitting at a table with him was going to push hard on my dubious self-control, and that was a really dumb thing to try hungry. "I just came to load up a plate. I have to get back to my room." To do what, I had no bloody idea—but the next time I encountered Devan Lovatt, I intended to have my game face on, shoes on my feet, and food in my belly.

"Sure." He tossed a soft bun that landed on top of the rest of my food. "There will be a full table here all day if you get hungry again. Travel lag can be hell on meal schedules."

Apparently, he'd been off planet—that was really unusual for colonists. The Federation tended to keep them solidly on local terra firma, especially those who would one day rule. Avoiding contamination.

I stopped in the doorway, suddenly loath to leave.

"You did a really nice thing with that kid yesterday—the one who ran into the girl and broke his toy."

"I did what anyone would do." He kept efficiently loading the plate in his hand.

"You didn't. You saw his heart, not the damage he caused. It matters."

He looked at me a moment. "Run into a few people in your time, have you?"

A lot more than a few. "You showed him kindness—he won't forget."

Devan set his plate down on the table and walked slowly over to join me. Every step he took increased the turbulence in the pit of my belly and the rat's nest in my Song. He slid to a halt in front of me and leaned casually against the wall. "You're not what I expected."

There was a lot of that going around. I took a jagged breath. "What were you expecting?"

He flashed a wry grin. "To be a lot more annoyed at the person who's come to convince me that Janelle is the love of my life."

His words were casual—friendly, even—but his notes sang potently of the man underneath. A combination of his father's charisma and his mother's fire, and the ability to hide both very well.

My Song saw him just fine—and it wanted. I wanted. Which was the fastest path to insanity and unemployment that I could possibly imagine. "You object to my mission?" I could hardly blame him.

"I know you're here at the Inheritor's request." He shrugged, face affable. "I don't expect you to succeed."

That was blunt. "Janelle shares your opinion."

"She's not easily swayed." His eyes were deep brown and opaque, no longer the friendly puppy dog. "Neither am I."

"I believe the first. I'll reserve judgment on the second." I had no idea why I needed to poke at him, but I did.

He laughed, and something just south of my belly button tied itself into a hot Cerulian knot. "You've met my parents. Twenty-six years of that, and I'm pretty good at not letting myself get pushed around."

That was becoming rapidly apparent. "I'm not here to force anyone into anything."

"Maybe not." He shrugged, a man comfortable with diplomatic wordsmithing. "But you're here to throw your weight on the scales."

I was. In service of the greater good, but that wasn't always much fun for the people who got leaned on. I hummed a quiet subsonic note, recognizing it as my own confusion. The two targets of this particular assignment were throwing me into a hell of a tangle. "You're the Inheritor Elect. You're already standing on a pretty weighted scale."

He raised an eyebrow. "You don't like Inheritors?"

I was way scattered if he'd been able to read that—I'd learned a long time ago to leave my free-wheeling digger roots well hidden. "My personal feelings don't matter here."

He snorted. "Like hell they don't."

They weren't supposed to, and when you worked for

KarmaCorp, that was basically the same thing. I gritted my teeth and tried not to scream at the flame-dancing harmonics of lust and desire having a wild party under my ribs. "I like to think that people can make themselves into who they want to be."

Which was a supremely stupid thing to have just said to a man I'd come here to lean on. I was one very messed-up Fixer.

He studied me for a long, quiet moment and then took a bite out of his bun. "Tell me about yourself, Singer."

Not a chance. "This isn't about me."

"You're here to try to weld my ass to the chair my parents want me to sit in." The imperial blood in his veins was suddenly very obvious. "So I'm damn well making it about you. I like to know a little bit about people I might have to punch in the nose."

I had to laugh, and that settled my harmonics some. "You might have to get in line behind Janelle."

He snorted. "If she's throwing punches, I won't need to."

The affection was mutual, then. My Song spiked more notes of confusion—affection was generally only a very small step away from love. What the heck was keeping these two apart? "It sounds like you like her."

"I do." His grin was quick, self-deprecating, and utterly lethal. "Don't get your hopes up, it won't make your job any easier."

I knew the answer already—even my jangling Talent

could read the obvious—but I asked anyhow. "You don't want to marry her?"

"No." The same simple, clear answer she'd given. "We kissed once when we were eight. There's nothing there. I like her very much, but there's no fire."

Plenty married with less than mutual affection. I tried desperately to yank my thoughts away from visions of kissing the Inheritor Elect of a planet I'd never visit again. "You think fire's necessary?"

His smile was a little wistful. "Yeah, I do. My parents have it. So do hers."

On the digger rock I'd grown up on, life had been hard for everyone, but it had been far harder for some. Those who thrived generally did it on the strength of either big hate or big love. Heat and passion, either way.

Which were the last things I should be thinking about right now. I punched the subsonic notes of my Talent again, this time hitting my guts with quick, tight orders. *Behave.*

Devan smiled and moved back to the table and his half-filled plate. He stuck his fork into the plate of bacon and then looked back up to where I still stood, a statue in the doorway. "I won't wish you luck, Lakisha Drinkwater. But it's good to have met you."

I turned and slowly walked away, trying not to drop my bacon or the few shreds of composure I had left.

I'd survived. I'd held my own, been as professional as I knew how to be in my bare feet, and managed not to jump into Devan Lovatt's lap. Given the current state of my insides, I was going to call that a success.

Now I just needed several hours in a dark, cold, isolated cave. I looked both ways as two hallways intersected and scooted in the direction of my rooms.

"Singer."

The single word stopped me before I'd made it three steps down the last leg of my retreat. I turned slowly, taking deep breaths as I went.

Evgenia looked me up and down and sniffed, particularly at my bare toes. My new host, doing her lady-of-the-manor thing.

I had to give her credit—it was a very nice manor. I called on every gram of the discipline KarmaCorp had tried to beat into my head over the last fifteen years. "Good morning, Madame Inheritor."

"And to you." She nodded her head in brief greeting. "I was hoping to find you." Her eyes glanced at the plate still clutched in my clammy hands and then back up at me, unwilling amusement glinting in their depths. "I see that my son got to you first."

She was a woman who didn't miss much. "He was kind enough to give me a brief tour. You lay out an impressive breakfast."

"We aim to please."

I was pretty sure she did that about as often as I donned high heels and sat in a spacer's lap. "In that case, consider me a well-satisfied guest." Or one who would be headed that way once I had a chance to wolf down the contents of my plate.

"I'm glad you're enjoying our food." She smiled at me, widow spider to foolish prey. "I've arranged a small dinner party for this evening in honor of your arrival. Our neighbors will wish to welcome you to Bromelain III."

She made it sound more likely that they'd want to run me out of town on the business end of a blaster. "That's very kind of you, but I generally like to keep a low profile while I'm working."

"You would be far more conspicuous in your absence," she said smoothly. "Although if it's a low profile you seek, you may wish to wear shoes to the event."

My bare toes curled up in embarrassment before I forced them back out again. I wasn't a nursling brat to be chastised—I was a Singer, and a damn fine one. I held back the growl rising in my throat. "I imagine I can find a pair by then."

She acknowledged my parry with the barest tilt of her head. "If you experience any difficulty, just let a member of my staff know. They would also be happy to fill you a breakfast plate in future, should you so desire."

The woman knew how to wield a delicate and vicious sword. I said nothing. Sometimes silence was a very useful weapon.

Her chin tipped two centimeters higher. "Dinner will be at dusk on the outside patio. Formal wear and dancing."

If she thought she could embarrass a miner's brat with a formal dinner, she was a thousand lightyears away from right. Trainees were thoroughly schooled in basic cultural graces and the skills to meld seamlessly into whatever society we landed in. I was no Dancer, but I wouldn't be embarrassed by a couple of turns around a patio or by a neighborly dinner, even if it came with five forks.

Which, I realized belatedly, Evgenia would likely know. There was more to her agenda here than trying to make me trip over my own toes. I capitulated—for now. "I enjoy dancing. It will be my pleasure to attend."

"The Inheritor will be pleased to hear it." She turned to go, and missed the flash of surprise I couldn't hide. I had assumed the dinner was her idea, but the harmonics were clear. She was merely the messenger, albeit an obnoxiously regal one.

I rocked back on my bare heels, realigning my math. Evgenia's motives in all of this were murky and hard to understand, but Emelio's intentions seemed obvious—put the putative lovebirds together in the same room and see what the Singer can do.

I couldn't fault his tactics—and perhaps they would help me out of the unholy mess I'd dug myself into. I assumed the blaster-carrying neighbors would be adequate incentive to stay out of the Inheritor Elect's lap —and maybe observing Janelle and Devan side-by-side would let me find a way through this that I sure as heck couldn't lay eyes on at the moment.

A way that wouldn't make me feel like intergalactic scum.

13

FINALLY, a face I recognized—which might be a good thing, or not. I made my way through the gathering throngs of people on the Lovatt compound's main lawn, ignoring the open curiosity and pointed stares. Tameka stood just inside the front gates, surveying the crowd.

I wanted to say hello—and I needed to know why she'd come. "I didn't expect to see you here."

She nodded at me and smiled, her face wearing the bland look of diplomats everywhere. "I believe the dinner invitation went out to all the neighbors."

Judging from the number of people who had arrived with overnight bags, "neighbors" was a very loose term. I reached up to my temples, already feeling the grinding inside. The last thing I needed right now was another Fixer on an intercept course.

A brief touch of something warm, and the aching under my fingers subsided.

I looked at Tameka in surprise, recognizing the vibrations of a trained Talent. Her fingers were shaping the air in front of her into a gentle figure eight. Soothing. Smoothing. She smiled at me. "Whatever else I may be, Lakisha Drinkwater, I'm not your enemy."

She wasn't—my Song could hear that just fine. But she might be something even more dangerous. "Sorry. It's been a really long couple of days." Ones where I'd spent way too much time apologizing and not nearly enough getting my job done.

Tameka was watching me with interest. "Something's still shaking you."

Not anything I was prepared to talk about—and not anything I wanted her to see. "It won't affect my ability to work."

"Park the attitude, child. I'm not Yesenia."

I wasn't a child, but arguing that point would just make me feel like one. I dug around for a safer subject. "I tried bacon."

Her face creased in a huge and genuine smile. "Ah, one of our special treats—how did you like it?"

"I ate three platefuls at lunch." Which had caused minor stomach protestations, but they'd been entirely worth it.

She chuckled and pointed at a rotund gentlemen sitting on a bench with a lady on each knee. "Ronald will be very happy to hear it. He's in charge of most of Bromelain III's pigs. He'd be glad to take you out to meet his charges, if you like."

I'd grown up on a mining rock—it still made me squirm to find out where my food came from, especially if it was mobile. "I think I'll just wait until they're turned into bacon, thanks."

Her eyes twinkled. "Spoken like a dumb flatlander."

I sobered quickly—there was no way that choice of words had been accidental, and I would do well to remember that this wily old woman didn't Dance on my team. "You talked to Janelle."

"Yes." No hesitation. "She likes you. I consider her a good judge of character."

Figuring out the good guys and the bad guys on this planet was going to split my head in two. "I like her too."

"That's going to make your job harder."

That, and my idiot hormones. "A Fixer who expects her work to be easy is doomed to be disappointed." It was one of those axioms they drilled into us in trainee school —and it annoyed me just as much now as it had then.

Tameka snorted. "A Fixer who spouts drivel doesn't last long working for Yesenia Mayes."

I raised an eyebrow and tried a diplomatic stare of my own. "You seem to know an awful lot about my boss for someone who lives on a backwater planet."

Her lips quirked. "You do that very well."

I wasn't sure that was a compliment.

"Relax," she said quietly. "I imagine this assignment has thrown you for a bit of a loop, but this evening is something you know how to do. Watch. Observe. Collect data."

Just like I'd told the third-year trainees. I met her gaze as directly as I could. Whatever side of the fence she might be riding tonight, it was good advice—from someone who'd done this job for longer than I'd been alive. "So, what do I need to know to survive this shindig?"

She smiled. "Strong opinions are appreciated, folks tend to go by their first names, and the amber stuff in the martini glasses is homebrewed and lethal."

Good to know. "Noted."

She paused a moment. "And at some point, go tell Ronald you like his bacon. He's got a lot of pull on this planet, and you could use a friend or two that the Lovatts and Brookers can't boss around."

I glanced at the man who still had two nubile young women on his lap, hearing what the wily old Fixer hadn't said. "You like him?"

"I do." She shrugged, eyes twinkling. "Just don't sit on his knee."

That would happen exactly never.

Tameka took two frothy green drinks from a passing server and handed one to me. "Go mingle, Singer. Let them see what you're made of. Around here, that matters."

It did on a digger rock, too. I squared my shoulders and took a sip of frothy green. Pleasant and vaguely minty. "Thank you."

"Oh, you can decide later if you want to thank me." She toasted me with her drink and made to move off into the crowd. "Best of luck, Lakisha Drinkwater. I have a feeling you might need it."

I took another sip of my drink, both comforted and

disquieted, and bemused by a woman who could hand out both in a three-minute conversation.

And wondered exactly what game she was playing at tonight.

-ooo-

My eyes roamed the lawn, taking in the configurations, the informal shaping of a crowd that said much about power and influence and who hadn't gotten in a shower tube with enough frequency lately.

There were the usual folks traveling in the center, the suns around which lots of minor planetary types found their orbits. Smaller groupings on the periphery, some there by choice or habit, some because they hadn't yet gotten permission to enter into a sun's orbit and believed permission was needed. A few travelers wandering solo, although in this crowd, relatively few.

I let my Talent roam quietly, reading base notes and harmonies, noting off-key slides and chromatics. Not a lot of those here—Bromelain III was a pretty straightforward place. Its Song would have strong notes, a clear melody line, and lots of people very intentionally moving to a beat of their own.

A colony of folks who prized their freedom. Not a place where I'd expect to find a lot of support for an arranged marriage, no matter what the StarReaders had seen in their cards and charts. This was the kind of planet where people built their own destinies and were happy to do it.

And yet the guy running the place had sent for a Fixer. I looked around again, keeping my eye out for the key players. I had a rough read of the land—now I needed to see how the terrain responded to the people at the core of this particular assignment.

A stir at the left edge of the crowd had me turning, even as my Talent recognized the shifting notes, the new melodic influence. Emelio—and right behind him, a smiling, sunny Devan.

My gut clenched, even as my Song reached out in greeting. I yanked it back with both hands and all the discipline I could scare up on short notice. I wasn't here to woo the man to my bed. My hormones hadn't been this out of control since I'd come out of a cryo-sleep trip two years ago with a body that believed it had missed a decade of sex.

Using the kind of language that would make even a digger-rock mother blush, I read myself the riot act in short, sharp sentences. Then I tucked whatever insanity was rising in my Song away in a nuclear bunker, threatened it with blaster fire if it so much as twitched, and turned my attention back to the warm evening, the people collected on the Lovatt lawn, and the way the music had changed the moment the Inheritor and his son had landed.

Because *damn*, had it changed. And not entirely in ways I would have imagined.

The respect for Emelio was clear, and in most cases it came with a healthy dose of personal affection. The man connected with his people. The Song of the crowd had shifted to put him at the core, and it had done so without pissing off the people who had just been displaced on center stage. Which was a remarkable accomplishment for a man who looked like he did little more than smile and shake hands all day.

The swirls around Devan were what fascinated me most, though. Some respect for his position as Emelio's metaphorical right hand, but a surprising amount for the man himself. Affection, too. But more, there were quiet lines of discontent on his behalf, and unspoken promises in the event that the man in question ever decided to make any moves off his father's shoulder. Not a revolt—it didn't have that kind of flavor at all. Just the support of some very independent and opinionated colonists for a young man they liked very much.

It tugged on something deep in my belly. I liked him too.

More stirring, this time on the northern edge of the lawn. I read Janelle's presence before I saw her. She stepped into my line of sight moments later and flashed me a cheery wave.

The neighbors who had moved to flank her startled, and then fell into formation around her anyhow. A couple sent me dirty looks, but most just settled into greeting each other and raiding passing food trays, their message sent. Janelle's parents might be off-planet, but they wanted me to know she didn't walk alone.

I wondered if they understood just how little she needed their help. I shook my head—the StarReaders didn't goof pretty much ever, but anyone who thought this woman could be gently nudged needed to get out of their office and spend some time in the presence of real-live human beings.

That line of thought felt good for about five seconds, and then I remembered it was my job to be the one who got out of the office and did actual work. I sighed, grabbed a tiny pastry that smelled like bacon and eggs, and turned up the volume dial on my Talent. I must be missing something. I'd been sent here because the powers-that-be thought a Singer's nudges would work. Whatever reputation we might have in some parts of the galaxy, Fixers very rarely forced anything—it not only ran against our ethics, but it generally didn't work very well either. We leaned, we influenced, we shifted the tides under things that were already there.

Carefully, I cleared my mind of anything but sound and sent out tonings, the listening radar pings of Talent that would hear the subtle undercurrents, the quiet hints of story traveling far underground. Most Singers couldn't do this kind of work in a crowd, but I'd grown up learning how to dig through rock and muck and hard places. The data flowing on the Lovatt lawn reformed and sharpened as I listened. Carefully, I let the notes of what I found resonate against what I'd already heard.

And didn't like what they said to me at all.

I finally backed out of my deep listening trance, well aware it had been a dumb thing to do on a lawn full of people, especially with a decent number of them poised to be unfriendly or downright hostile. And it hadn't netted me much to work with. A hundred people to gather intel from, and there was still nothing of substance supporting any kind of romantic connection between Devan and Janelle. A few wry hopes for the partnership of the two of them—but none with any real heart energy.

Whatever the StarReaders had charted, the people of Bromelain III didn't see it.

Which left me with very few allies on this grass—and my targets had a waiting army if they ever chose to use it. However much respect the residents of BroThree had for Emelio Lovatt, and it was substantial, they would not support his plan here, or my work.

I was going to be Singing very much alone.

-ooo-

"Singer."

Devan's voice at my shoulder caught me by surprise—and my jumpy evasive maneuver nearly ran me into Janelle, coming up on my other side.

She grinned and slung an arm through mine. "Evening, Kish."

Flanked. I hadn't even heard them coming. "Fancy meeting you two here."

Janelle chuckled and steered us around a large group of gawking people. I ground my teeth and tried not to kick both of them in the shins. No one on this planet had any idea what low profile looked like.

I had just become an actress in a two-bit play—one who didn't know her part. New music started up, and I decided it was time to improvise. I cast a sweet look up at

Devan, hoping he could see the hints of murder in my eyes. "It's a lovely night. You and Janelle should dance."

The woman in question snorted and sent me a wry look. "You'll have to be a lot more subtle than that, Singer."

I waved politely at the audience avidly watching us. "We're being subtle, are we?"

Both of them laughed.

I relaxed a little—apparently, I'd managed my lines well enough. Janelle angled us over to a copse of trees. "Sorry. We're being a little obnoxious."

They had good reason, but that wasn't making their shins any safer.

Devan motioned at a couple of nearby staffers, ensuring us relative privacy and reminding me he was planetary royalty, all in one quick, easy move. "You've been watching us all night. Care to tell us what data you're storing away in that busy head of yours?"

The KarmaCorp operations manual screeched in protest. I ignored it—it hadn't exactly been making itself useful on this assignment. And something in his tone had me snared. "You both have widespread support here, and there is very little for the Inheritor's position on your marriage."

His eyebrows flew up in surprise—whether at the information or at my honesty, I couldn't tell.

"Told you." Janelle's voice carried tones of easy affection. "They support the man and the office, not every harebrained idea he comes up with."

I jumped to Emelio's defense, well aware my motives

were murky at best. "It seems like a fairly well-considered way to maintain harmony between the two most important families on this planet." I threw my hands up as they both turned on me. "I'm not saying it's the best idea, or the only one—but I don't think it's harebrained, either."

This time it was Janelle raising an eyebrow. "It doesn't sound like the people of Bromelain III agree with you."

They didn't—but the StarReaders agreed with Emelio. And I'd just made my job a whole lot harder by telling them the first when I couldn't tell them the second.

I'd never been so tempted to violate Ears Only in my entire life.

I looked into Devan's eyes, glad against all reason that I'd told him that the people of this planet had his back. And wished, with all my heart, that I could tell him why I couldn't do the same.

"I spoke with Tameka." Janelle sounded like she was discussing the upcoming apple harvest. "She said you wouldn't use force."

My demon child lit, offended and furious. "I already promised you that."

Devan inserted his bulk between us with surprising swiftness.

Janelle pushed him aside, temper flaring—and then slid to a halt, eyes beaming apology. She laid a quiet hand on my arm, and a cautioning one on his. "Yes, you already did. I'm sorry, I didn't mean to question your integrity."

How could I not like someone who apologized that easily and that well? I sighed. "It's a valid question."

"So was yours the other day." She met my gaze steadily. "You asked me whether I would do this if it were good for my home, my people. I've been thinking about that."

Storm clouds gathered on Devan's face as he listened. "You didn't tell me that part."

She rolled her eyes at him. "I don't tell you everything, hot stuff. I can take care of myself. And I figure Kish has reasons for asking that she can't tell us."

I held my breath as she stepped toward the cusp of something I could nudge in entirely good conscience.

"No." Devan's words were quiet, but fierce temper kicked underneath them. "My parents have been working that line for twenty-six years, and in the end, what's good for Bromelain III comes down to a matter of opinion." His eyes were boring into mine. "If you know something we don't, now is a really good time to say so."

I couldn't. I knew too much, and far too little. I knew *how* the StarReaders had voted, but I didn't know *why*—and it was the latter we all needed right now. I took a deep breath, knowing battle lines had just been drawn and hating which side of them I stood on. "I've told you everything I can, and quite a few things I probably shouldn't have."

He nodded, eyes sad. "Yeah. I figured that."

"Think about it," I said softly. "Please."

"I have. For more years than you can probably imagine." He reached out a hand to Janelle. "I will always do what is best for my home and my people. But for better or worse, I have to be the person who decides what that is."

Janelle stepped to his shoulder, arm around his waist. She didn't say a word.

She didn't have to. I knew what I was looking at. A united front, one backed by a brick wall of unswerving loyalty an arm-span thick.

I had enough Talent to blast a brick wall to smithereens—but they were right. Neither KarmaCorp's ethics nor my own would ever let me use it.

I'd have to find a way around.

It wouldn't be the first time I'd done that on assignment, but this time it was going to make my guts bleed. I liked these two a whole lot, and that was wildly dangerous territory, especially with a man who made my hormones buzz. I could hear my KarmaCorp instructors in my head, warning of the neon dangers of personal entanglement—the loss of perspective, losing sight of the greater good in the face of real human desires and the good people who had them.

I'd listened to them, I really had.

I'd just never landed in that mud quite this thoroughly—and it was sucking my heart out through my boots.

-ooo-

I pasted myself against a tree trunk, watching couples dancing under the light of BroThree's twin moons, and tried mightily to keep the Song inside me tamped down tight. Letting it fly would give everyone in three kilometers a hell of a headache, and it likely wouldn't make me feel one iota better.

I could read the signs well enough. One Singer knocked way off her rocker. My chakras hadn't been this whacked since I was fourteen.

The trio in the corner of the lawn played lovely music on lute, viola, and some sort of percussive cylinder. Their subtle, skilled harmonies mocked me.

Harmony wasn't within my reach tonight.

I hummed a basic rebalancing chant, cringing at the out-of-tune reverberations. Even the tree at my back seemed to wince. I activated my subsonics, looking to dampen the whole mess—and then gave up as I saw Janelle and Devan again and felt my insides slide even further out of whack. The two of them had made their way out into the clear area of lawn that was serving as tonight's dance floor. She swung into his arms with a smooth grace that suggested they'd done this many times before, and started chatting away like two entirely platonic neighbors who knew what the fates intended for them and couldn't care less.

I pushed my subsonics their direction, thoroughly annoyed at act two of their little play. And sighed when the echoes came back. They weren't acting. Gorgeous music, twin moons hanging in a mystical sky, and the only one feeling the romance was me.

I turned a cranky eye to the sky and moons, about to give up and lock myself in a handy dungeon for the night, and then reconsidered. Devan and Janelle were expecting an attack on their brick wall—but I knew the benefits of a carefully placed drill. The flares of teal and gold overhead just might be a good place to start.

I opened my higher chakras, the ones that reach upward to spirit, to emotion, to those things we can't quite see but know to be true, and gathered that energy into the beginnings of melody.

I frowned as the notes shaped themselves. Way too damn fragile and ethereal for what I needed—drills needed substance. I reached for the percussive beat from the musical trio, smiling as my forming Song took on a far firmer shape. Better. Much better.

I had a foundation now, and lots of easy material to build with. Next, I sought out the notes of romance in the dancing crowd. An old couple over to the left, rocking to the gentle, steady love of a lifetime. Two dancers with fast feet and appreciative eyes, feeling out how they moved together. A very pregnant woman, Devan's oldest sister unless I missed my guess, swaying with a man's arms wrapped around her belly. A young girl sitting under a bush with two friends, testing out the wobbly legs of her first crush. I didn't change their songs any—they were beautiful just as they were. I only augmented their signal some, boosted the acoustics.

And then I turned back to my errant couple, satisfied with the Song I'd built. Time for some flanking maneuvers of my own. We'd see how well their stubborn heads held up against well-crafted Talent.

Devan and Janelle were still gliding through the

simple shapes of whatever dance this was, feet on autopilot as they moved and talked.

Good. They'd let their guard down, as had everyone else. No one was paying any attention to the cranky Fixer under a tree. I wasn't harboring any illusions—both of the people in my sights would be utterly furious if they knew what I was about to try next.

It wouldn't break my promise to Janelle, but it would skirt damn close.

I closed my eyes, readying.

And then, ever so lightly, I wrapped my song of ethereal, pulsating romance around the two of them, light as a feather.

Something in my heart keened.

I blasted it with pure heat. I was a girl from a digger rock—I knew better than to pine after things I couldn't have.

I sent my melody of romance and wooing up Janelle and Devan's musical currents, looking for cracks. Tiny crevices, ones where I could maybe give a note a little more resonance, a harmonic a slightly more tuned pitch. The lightest of touches, seeking a place for my drill to land.

Their crevices pushed back.

I gripped the tree behind me and snarled, patience suddenly and irrevocably gone. I wasn't the best Singer in this quadrant for nothing. Dialing up the nozzle on my Talent, I leaned harder, put more demand into my quest for a chink in their united armor.

I wasn't asking them to frolic on the lawn naked, for

fuck's sake. I just wanted them to *look*. To see each other with eyes that hadn't been trained by twenty-five years of familiarity—to see each other as I saw them. A woman who could be a friend. A man I could love.

A man I could love.

My Song exploded, notes skittering away into the dancing, starry sky. I cringed into the tree at my back, holding on to its solidness for dear life as the careening remnants of my melody shrieked and rended.

Spaceships had torn in two with less noise.

And when I could finally lift my head again, I wanted nothing more than to be that spaceship. I could feel the panic rising from my root chakra right up to the tips of my hair. The catastrophe had been silent to all ears but mine, but a catastrophe it was, nonetheless.

My Talent had failed—and it had been done in by my own base notes rising up in mutiny.

14

FINALLY. I breathed fully for the first time in hours as the last of the lights of the Lovatt compound dimmed behind me. I had waited until every last guest had gone, offered every polite smile and gracious word I had in me to give. I'd nodded politely at Devan when he included me in conversation, and agreed to join Janelle for a horse-back ride in the morning.

I barely knew what a horse was, but every gram of self-preservation I had left had simply been trying to survive the current minute and the one after that.

The minutes were finally done. And now I could let what had broken inside me rise and be free. I had no choice but to let it out. My Talent had failed, and that was the kind of problem that killed missions.

A Singer can't sing against her own will. I'd powered through my own distaste, dislike, and some really foul moods on previous assignments, but always, *always* I'd been able to lean on the one truth that is soaked into every Fixer's DNA. Do the job. Act for the greater good, whatever your personal reactions. Trust KarmaCorp. I didn't Sing blindly—but somewhere, I'd always been able to dig up that faith.

Until now.

I filled my lungs, feeling my breath hitch and the winds curl around me in reply. I'd come to the right place. These grasslands called to me, even when my heart and Talent were in total disarray.

I felt my legs leap into action, answering the call, carrying me beyond the edges of manicured civilization and out into the sweeping sea of grass. My churning legs bolted far into the night and the rustling waves, trusting that the grasses would bring me back again when I needed them to. I would never be lost here—not physically, anyhow.

The stalks closed in around me, murmuring quiet sympathy. I sang them a few quick, pissy notes. This was not my planet, and they were not my grasses. Answer rippled from organisms that traced their DNA from long before the first humans began. They belonged to no one, to everyone, just like the stars over my head.

I sighed and slowed down my wild run. My parents hadn't understood the child they'd taken in, but they'd always let me move my legs. On an inner planet I'd have landed in the office of a well-meaning psychologist, but miners had never found me deal-breaking strange—hanging out in dark tunnels for forty-eight hours straight tends to rejigger your definition of sane.

My lungs heaved, protesting the late-night exercise.

And my Song strained, fighting the stranglehold I'd set on it the moment I first laid eyes on Devan Lovatt. It was time to let it loose, to give time and space and oxygen to whatever inside me had tried to run my Talent into the side of an asteroid this night.

Time to let my soul speak its truth in the most honest way I knew how—even if I quaked at hearing what it had to say. I stopped my feet, knowing I could run forever and not get away from what I carried inside me. The demon child had tried.

The first notes rose up the instant my bare toes planted in dirt. Weightless, soaring high ones that would be audible far above the waving grasses. My lament to the stars. No subsonics this time—this was a Song that needed to be heard.

I reached down to earth and up to sky and let the wild energy in my ribs go. Music exploded out, great rending runs of notes and aching, fragile ones. Chromatics that made my ears wince, and harmonies so beautiful, I could hardly stand to let them go.

A cacophony of sound and meaning—and very little of it made any sense at all.

I took a deep breath and let the notes fade, shaking my head ruefully. I felt like I'd flown through three lightyears of space shrapnel without a suit. There was a reason we were supposed to Sing every day. Even a first-year trainee knew the basic exercises to keep Talent degunked and chakras unglued. It was long past time for some Singer basic nutrition.

I reached out both hands for the grasses at my sides

and joined their swaying, letting the cool earth beneath my toes and the starkissed light on my forehead shape a loop. Anchoring into that flow, I let my base note rise up the center of my spine, listening as it passed each of my chakras. Noticing the resonances and the lack of them.

Not fixing, yet—just listening.

I let the note that was entirely, purely me rise all the way up to my braids. And then I tipped my head up to the starry night and let a sad, wry chuckle limp out. "You are one heck of a mess, Lakisha Drinkwater."

The grasses around me murmured their agreement.

I pushed my toes deeper into the dirt and began with my root chakra, singing the low, resonant notes that would call it back into alignment. That one shifted easily enough—it always had. Rocks were hard to unbalance overmuch.

I worked my way up, Singing to the nodes of energy in my spine as I went. My heart chakra quivered, but settled into place with a little tender underpinning. It was my throat chakra that balked entirely.

I had things to say—and it wasn't going to go quietly into the night or into alignment until I said them.

I sighed and stopped trying to placate it with simple harmonics.

The music that rose out of me this time was less wild, less chaotic. Meaning lived there now, stories I could hear and understand. Stories I needed to honor, no matter what I chose to do with them next.

I breathed in and listened to my own truth, Sung as best as I knew it. Layers of frustration and hurt, emanating, as always, from the edges of a demon child who never felt quite worthy and a woman who had never felt entirely comfortable as a cog. Notes I knew well.

I swam deeper, seeking what it was that my soul needed me to hear this night. And found it in the yearning. In the wanting. In the small, reverberating undertones that held tight to stardust and romance and didn't want to let go.

Fragile, ethereal notes. Ones that had never met the business end of a drill.

I let them out, tears rolling down my cheeks.

The grasslands offered soothing, lullabies of ease and comfort. I kicked my Song out at them. Comfort wasn't what I sought this night.

They kicked back and almost made me laugh— planets don't take much shit. This one didn't have any tolerance for my self-pity.

I didn't care. Sometimes, we puny humans need to feel things even when the wiser entities of the galaxy find us foolish.

I let my Song range back to the aching high notes it had begun with. A soprano's lament, sung to grasses and stars that would hear and hold my truth long after I ceased to exist. Devan Lovatt wasn't mine to have. Even if the StarReaders hadn't already cast their vote, I was a Fixer. I'd never visit BroThree again, and he was this planet's ruler-in-waiting.

I broke the music off in mid-note, cursing. I was sounding like some hapless heroine in a romance novel, dammit.

I let go and charged out into the dark, grassy waves again, feeling them grasp at my running feet and then give way. I'd run like this in the tunnels as a child, and one insanely memorable time, on the asteroid's surface. A demon child in an astrosuit, feet pounding on the surfaces of the rock she called home.

Alone beneath the stars. Just like tonight.

My lungs heaved in the air of Bromelain III, protesting the exertion. I was no longer the child who had traveled all her days at breakneck speeds. I was the woman that child had chosen to become, and that woman didn't want to break her neck on a backwater planet over a man she couldn't have.

The grasses murmured as I dropped back to a walk, my breath rasping out from lungs that had been caught by surprise too many times tonight. I reached into my bag for water to soothe my throat.

And then, with a discipline that would have astonished my trainers, I pulled on the cloak of responsible adult. I let my breathing settle. I set my Song loose long enough to wail her last lines one more time and then reeled her back, smiling a little as the sulky, miffed final notes settled into place.

My throat chakra was sore as all hell, but it was back in a nice tight line with all the others. I had listened. I had allowed my truth its moment on earth and under sky.

Maybe now it would stay out of the way while I did the job I'd come here to do.

15

A DECENT NIGHT'S sleep can set the whole world right again. Or not.

I looked over at Janelle, who was seated on a creature identical to mine and looking entirely at home there. "This is nuts—you know that, right?" I'd ridden a digging drill down a five-hundred-meter mineshaft with half my safety tethers loose, and that hadn't felt nearly this crazy.

"You said you loved the grasslands, and like I told you last night, this is the best way to see them."

I had no memory of that conversation.

She leaned over and patted the neck of the beast I sat on. "Don't worry. Dusty here is as mild-mannered as horses come. All the kids around here use him to learn to ride."

I stuck my right foot in the thing that looked like a medieval torture device and tried to find some kind of comfortable way to sit. "Apparently, I'm just a dumb flatlander."

Her laugh pealed out over Dusty's ears. "You kind of look like one at the moment."

I looked like hell warmed over. That much I'd verified before I'd slammed on a hat and slithered out to greet the dawn.

Janelle tipped her head a little, regarding me closely. "You okay?"

"I'm fine. Just plotting my revenge when you visit my digger rock."

She grinned. "I have four brothers—I don't scare easily."

Most days, I didn't either. I stuck out my tongue at her smart-ass face, feeling better despite my best efforts—and then yanked it back in again as she kicked her horse's sides and we started to move.

It was like straddling the top of a really wide, rumbly mountain. I held on tight with my knees and wished deeply for a proper tether. "This is a secret plot to leave my bones out rotting in some grassy field, isn't it?"

"No." She smiled over her shoulder. "But that would've been a good idea."

Fixers sometimes died on assignment, but I refused to be remembered as the one who expired while riding a four-legged senior citizen. I held on tighter with my knees, and then grabbed for anything my hands could reach as Dusty sped up.

Janelle leaned over and snagged one of the leather steering straps as we roared by. "Whoa, easy there, big guy." She looked over at me and rolled her eyes. "If you grip that hard, you'll be halfway around the planet by lunch, and you'll never walk again. Our horses are all trained to respond to pressure commands from your legs. Relax."

That sounded about as smart as letting go of a digger drill's handles. "If I do that, what keeps me attached to this creature?" The ground was a seriously long way down.

"Unity. Balance." She glanced sideways at me, still holding on to Dusty's steering line, her face full of mischief. "Isn't that what you KarmaCorp people are all about?"

I snorted and tried to relax my knees. "Not usually quite this literally."

"That's better." Janelle studied me with the eyes of an experienced teacher. "Relax your lower back, let it roll with his motions."

I did, and instantly felt better. "Ah. It's just like a digger drill." Go with the motion instead of fighting it.

"I'll take your word for it."

I wished she'd take my word for a few more things. "This is a really strange way of getting around."

"There are weirder." She smiled and looked out at the horizon. "Is it strange to travel so much? I've never lived anywhere but here."

I envied her sense of roots—ones I would likely never have. My life's work was to go wherever KarmaCorp sent me. "Lots of watching the walls of a tin can and knowing you could die at any minute."

Which made what I was doing now feel a little more sane. Horses probably didn't crash into too many asteroids. I stopped staring at the ground just in front of Dusty's nose and dared to look up.

The visual music of the grasslands hit me all at once, wide-open majesty as far as the eyes could see. Greens and browns and rich yellows, an aching tapestry that made me want to touch and dance and breathe and fly all at the same time.

They were an orchestra of song, these grasses. The large melodies of scale and grandeur, the tiny whispers of the individual blades and their feathery tops. The ones brushing against our feet set tiny ripples in motion, word of our passing traveling over the planetary skin. Just like miners in a drill shaft, there would always be the vibrations of a neighbor to keep you company.

It made me feel oddly homesick.

Which was foolish. Most digger-rock kids would run screaming from a big, sunny field of grass. I surely had, more times than anyone on Stardust Prime probably cared to remember. It had taken Tee's eternally patient father to teach me to appreciate wide-open spaces under the sun.

He would love the magic of this place.

I dropped my gaze back down to the safety of Dusty's brown-and-gold neck. I was still way out of sorts if I was missing both the mining rock of my childhood and the familiarity of my trainee years. Both had gotten under my skin plenty when they'd been my real life. A mission in disarray was no reason to be wishing for years that hadn't really been all that good or that simple.

It had never been easy to be a cog.

Janelle let go of Dusty's steering line, reached into a bag behind her leg, and pulled out a couple of apples. "Hungry?"

I was, but I wasn't sure I could spare any hands at the moment. Both of them were tightly wrapped in the long hair on Dusty's neck. "Maybe later."

She shrugged and dropped one back in the bag.

I looked at her two free hands suspiciously, attention solidly back in the present. "Shouldn't somebody be holding on to the steering devices?"

She looked puzzled and then picked up the line lying loosely on her horse's neck. "Oh, the reins? These are mostly for emergencies and beginners. Our horses are all trained to leg commands. My brothers and I used to jump on bareback without any equipment all the time."

That sounded like descending a shaft without safety tethers. "And where are your brothers buried?"

Her laughter seemed to amuse the grasses. "You were one of those safe and well-mannered kids, huh?"

That was almost as big an insult as calling me a dumb flatlander. "Nope. Total hellion."

"Really?" She tilted her head, regarding me with interest. "I can see that in you."

That pleased me more than it should. I looked around and grinned. "It was never this scenic, though. Or as high up."

The music of Janelle's laughter tugged at my Talent. Calling to friendship—and to foolishness.

Giving in to temptation, I picked up the whispering harmonies of the grasses around us and wove them into

Dusty's amiable, simple melody. The soothing rhythm of clopping feet, rolling yellow-green waves, and a planet's breath—accompanied by the slightly off-key notes of the woman holding on for dear life.

My mount flicked his ears back and forth.

Janelle smiled. "He likes it."

Great. I was the best Singer in the quadrant—and I was singing to a horse.

I dialed up my Talent a notch. Might as well knock Dusty's socks off. I added the subsonics gingerly—trainee school hadn't covered horses, and I didn't want this one deciding to leave me in a ditch somewhere.

His ears twitched faster. I hoped that was a good sign.

Janelle rode easily as I sang, amused by the horses and by me. And when I finished, she gave me a long, slow look. "I've been doing some thinking."

I pulled some of my brain out of composing sonnets to a horse. "That sounds serious."

She looked carefully away from me, eyes scanning the horizon. "I'm reconsidering my position on Devan."

Ease fled.

She took a bite of the apple in her hand and eyed me. "I'm wondering whether you and that singing of yours might have had anything to do with it."

I gulped and told the truth as best as I knew it. "I don't think so." That I'd tried didn't count—it hadn't worked. My Talent had blown up in my face. And I hadn't smelled so much as a whiff of interest from either of them before it had.

She raised an eyebrow. "You promised not to mess with my knickers."

I looked down pointedly. "They still seem to be on."

She contemplated me for a while, and then she sighed. "It's too easy to forget that I need to be careful with you."

I wished, hard, that she didn't need to be. "I'm sorry."

"I think you are. That doesn't make this any easier."

I tried to offer her what I could. "Singers work with what already exists." If I'd gotten anywhere, it had been because something in her was willing to shift.

She raised a dubious eyebrow.

I wasn't remotely in the mood for a debate about Fixer ethics. "Look. The two of you are as stubborn as space rocks. If you think I've managed to lead you around by the nose, then go ahead and think it."

Some of the clouds on her face cleared. "You're easier to trust when you're pissy."

Dammit, why did I have to like these people? "He's a really good guy." I had no idea whether I was speaking as Fixer, friend, or woman who yearned.

"Yeah." She glanced over my way again. "You got me thinking, asking whether it would be good for my home and the people I love." Her cheeks flushed a little. "That's probably a really unromantic reason to be considering this."

The lines of duty and personal entanglement tightened around my throat. My Talent was hearing clear, steady truth in the words. She really was considering it. And it wasn't whiffs of magic and starlight in the DNA of her new notes—it was the leaning of a heart who cared deeply for her home and her planet and was willing to consider possibilities. A woman weighing the greater good, even if she could only sense it dimly.

I hadn't lied to her, then—my Talent hadn't swayed her. But maybe the words of a friend had.

Nausea rose in my throat, unbidden and harsh. She was shifting, moving in a direction I could use. My Talent could see the way.

It was my heart that wavered.

16

THE INVITATION for late-morning tea on the terrace had been phrased as a request. I was quite sure that it wasn't one. Today wasn't going to tread lightly, no matter what my pounding head might prefer.

I tottered after the slight woman who had fetched me out onto the terrace, stumbling over invisible bumps on the perfectly smooth floor. Staying on Dusty had been an experience. Getting off him had been sheer hell. My legs were making it clear that they intended to complain for at least a decade.

The rest of me didn't have that long. I needed to get my shit together, preferably in the next three seconds. The Inheritor would be seeking an update, and the last thing I needed right now was him getting a sniff at the current state of either my assignment or my heart.

Emelio turned his head slightly as I came into view. "Good morning, Singer. I trust you slept well."

It was a simple pleasantry. I tried not to growl—or to

mention that I'd already been up for hours. "Your hospitality has been exemplary, thank you."

He indicated the chair beside him, positioned to look out over the sweeping vistas below. I sat gingerly, letting my eyes follow the swaying dance of the grasslands—and had to grudgingly admit they were better from horseback. Even if I wasn't going to walk right for days.

A server quietly removed plate covers and filled glasses on the trays beside us. Apparently this was more than a cup of tea.

"I had the staff bring us a late breakfast, as I haven't had a chance to eat yet." He smiled and unfolded his napkin. "And I've been told that you are fond of our bacon."

I suspected he'd been told a whole lot more than that. "Very much so." Just the smell of it was mellowing out the drumbeat in my head some.

"Tell me." Emelio picked up his fork, the dictionary definition of casual elegance. "How have you found our planet so far?"

I told the absolute truth. "The grasslands are glorious."

"They are." I could hear his pride—and his curiosity. "Have you watched them only from windows and balconies, or have you let the grasses brush your fingertips?"

A test—dumb flatlanders never went outside. "My grandfather used to say that until you've touched the rocks of a planet, you haven't really landed."

"He sounds like a wise man."

He'd been kind to a small child with a fierce temper. "He died when I was six." And at his request, been buried under a pile of rock.

"You miss him."

It hadn't been phrased as a question. I swallowed down the old, aching hurt—it wasn't relevant here, and I didn't need to give these people any more hooks into me than they already had. "I assume there's a reason you asked me to join you this morning."

He inclined his head slightly. "My wife and I are curious as to how your assignment is progressing."

I had a shredded heart and a chink in Janelle's brick wall that might actually help me get the job done, and both were making me sick to my stomach. None of which I intended to say to the man whose son was next up on my to-do list. "I imagine Evgenia wanted to be here to ask me that herself."

He paused, fork in mid-lift. "You're very direct."

I might have been born somewhere else, but I'd earned my digger-rock DNA fair and square. We had a strong preference for straight lines. "I don't enjoy wasting time."

"You would find my upcoming day very frustrating, then." He smiled. "I don't know what you've seen on other Inheritor planets, but here, we're quite informal. Once or twice a month, we hold open hours for the citizens of Bromelain III to contribute their thoughts and ideas and to air minor grievances. I will be in the hall of hearing this afternoon, listening."

He was right—I'd rather kill myself with a dull spoon.

I also assumed this conversational tangent wasn't accidental. "Will Devan be joining you?"

"Often, he does." Emelio refilled my glass of orange-colored juice that tasted of the tropics. "But when I peeked in earlier, those waiting are mostly the gray hairs, so today will be my turn. The older generations appreciate my own gray hair."

So much for a good excuse to hide in my room for the rest of the day. If Devan had been tucked away and inaccessible, I might have been able to justify it. "I imagine the ritual is pleasing for all of you."

He glanced at me as he topped up his own glass. "It's a way of life that is probably difficult for you to understand."

Fixers understood duty well enough—the comfort and the hell of it. "My roommate's from a family that has lived on Stardust Prime for ten generations. They've served KarmaCorp since it was formed. It gives them purpose and pride, and a place in the universe." Becoming a Singer had done the same for a blonde demon child who hadn't thought she mattered.

Emelio looked at me carefully. "I am Inheritor because I wanted to serve my people, and I believe deeply that stability at the top is a big part of what serves them."

I could hear the strength of his belief running deep and unshakeable below his words. The man might have a big ego, but he had a servant heart. "I bet it works better when the Inheritor isn't an asshole."

Emelio chuckled and regarded me with real warmth

for the first time. "I believe that was a compliment, my dear."

It had been. This mission would be a lot easier if I didn't like so many of the people involved. Even ones who were skillfully trying to herd me. I picked up my glass and took a sip of the orange froth. "Did you always want to be Inheritor?"

"I did. Which is fortunate, as I was an only child."

That wouldn't have been the intention—Inheritor families tried to have lots of fodder for future leadership roles. "You didn't feel pressured?"

"Of course I did." Emelio's eyes were dark and calm over the top of his glass. "But that is entirely different than being forced. I imagine that's something a Fixer might understand."

He was tricky, and definitely trying to herd me. And he was right. KarmaCorp didn't allow Talents to roam free in the world—but the choice to serve had been mine. Last night, my soul had lost sight of that. "A choice made under pressure can still be a choice."

The Inheritor bowed his head graciously, and kept silent.

A man who knew when to quit. A case very well made—and one that had tapped, with finesse and skill, into my own sense of duty. Inheritors weren't the only ones who served, or the only ones who gave up much to do so. "Thank you. This has been an interesting breakfast."

"Ones with my father usually are," said a dry voice behind me.

My head ramped back up into drumbeat overdrive.

"Good morning, son." Emelio's equanimity didn't shift a hair. "Join us for brunch?"

"Is that what this is?" Devan pulled up a chair and helped himself to some of the bacon on his father's plate. "No wonder there's none of this in the breakfast room." He grinned at me. "It's apparently all being routed to our honored guests."

The Inheritor forked the last of his bacon in a neat defensive maneuver. "And to those of us who will be working hard today."

"My day will be pure pleasure." Devan smiled at me. "My mother would like you to see more of Bromelain III. I've come to offer my services as tour guide."

I caught the traces of surprise on Emelio's face—and his bemused acceptance. Clearly, he hadn't known that his wife had machinations underway as well. He nodded blandly at his son. "That sounds like a wonderful idea."

I wasn't nearly as easy to herd as they all thought. I opened my mouth to say so—and then changed my mind. The next step in my assignment was clear. I had one crack for my drill. I needed to find another.

Waiting wasn't going to make looking for it any easier. My heart would mend back on Stardust Prime in my favorite ancient gel-chair with one of Tee's brews in my hand—and that wasn't going to happen until I got my job done. Sometimes you had to dig, ready or not. I pasted on a smile, met Devan's gaze, and threw my battered self to the wolves. "That would be lovely, thank you."

He grinned and stood up. "I'll get transpo ready and meet you downstairs."

I took a last swig of my tropical juice and breathed my spine straight. Just one small crack—that was all I needed to find. And then I could go home.

17

I WAS STARK RAVING MAD. I told myself so at least six times as I made my way over to the crushed-rock landing pad where a glittering silver b-pod waited. It was late model, real glass, and cost about as much as every transpo on my home rock put together.

The Inheritor Elect traveled in style.

I got a further shock when I stepped inside and discovered Devan at the helm. This size of cruiser generally came with a pilot, and a good one. "You're flying?"

"Sure." He grinned at me. "Unless you want to—Tameka says you've got a good hand with a stick."

Nobody put a ship like this into the hands of a near stranger. "For all you know, I've never driven anything bigger than a beetle." The littlest b-pods were dead simple to fly—most four-year-olds on a digger rock could manage well enough.

"Tameka keeps Nijinsky tuned pretty jumpy."

I'd noticed. Good pilots liked their rides to be really

responsive. The rest of the galaxy just wanted their transpo to head where they aimed. "Miners like their rigs jumpy—keeps us alive."

He nodded at the seat up front beside him. "Get much chance to fly working for KarmaCorp?"

Not on the books—Fixers were supposed to keep a low profile. "Officially my feet stay on the ground unless someone else is driving."

His lips twitched. "Noted."

Damn. I'd come here because I had a job to do, and because somewhere between the terrace and the landing pad I'd latched on to the desperate hope that getting to know Devan better would have the effect it usually did. Most guys had pimples if you opened your eyes wide enough, and it was hell on the attraction hormones.

In this case, hell was exactly what I needed—and not at all what I was getting.

A crack. I just needed one stinking, tiny crack. In him, and a few dozen less in me.

I felt the vibrations underneath us pick up as the b-pod lifted off the ground. A textbook take-off—maybe there was a reason his sister was a solar mechanic. Devan tapped a couple of touch screens and leaned back, a man in his element. "Okay, Ophelia, let's get out of here."

I was pretty sure he wasn't talking to me. "Ophelia?"

He grinned. "First girl my dad ever kissed."

Definitely a story there. "Does Evgenia know that?"

He laughed. "She named the ship."

I never wanted to meet either of his parents in a dark tunnel. "You have an interesting family."

"Yeah." Devan flew placidly over the edges of the Lovatt compound and then stepped on the gas and angled sharply up and left. Ophelia climbed steeply, and with the kind of pent-up energy that suggested she was just getting started.

I could practically feel my fingers twitching. She was tuned to be a pilot's dream.

He looked over at me, eyes full of simple happiness. "You want to fly her?"

I did, every millimeter of me—and I wasn't at all happy he knew that. "That would be a really bad idea."

His mouth twitched. "I doubt it."

"You should say no."

"Not gonna." He took his hands off the manuals. "All yours."

I'd spent the last few days fighting every primal urge I had—I wasn't going to fight this one. My hands were on the controls before either of us could blink or he could change his mind. Ophelia vibrated under my palms, saying hello. I rolled her a little, one side to the other. Returning the welcome.

Devan grinned beside me and tightened his straps.

I could have told him not to bother—Ophelia and I were going to fly smooth as silk. We had nothing but open skies and trailing winds, and she was as done with sedate as I was. "Okay if I bump up the speed a little?"

The man beside me chuckled.

I rolled my eyes. "You should say no."

"Not gonna."

That was as much permission as my pent-up demon

child needed. I pushed forward on Ophelia's throttles, feeling the purr and the roar sing through me. And realized I'd finally done something entirely right. This was *exactly* what I'd needed. I opened up to the power under my hands, feeling all my cranky, frazzled energy burn away in the pure pursuit of speed.

The grasslands waved underneath us, dancing with Ophelia's flight. I moved with the waves, pushing the ship through a zinging figure eight just because I could. And then laughed and drove straight for the horizon.

I had no idea how long it was before I came back to my senses and wistfully lifted my hands off the manuals. "Sorry—I don't know where we're going."

Devan smiled beside me and took over the controls. "No need to get there in a straight line."

Pretty sure we'd deep-sixed that flight plan. "Thanks. She's amazing to fly."

He was watching me from his seat, eyes full of curiosity and something deeper. "Your singing is beautiful."

I blinked. "What?"

He shrugged, looking a little uncomfortable. "You've got a really nice voice."

I hadn't intended to use it. I listened, sighing when I heard the fading subsonic echoes. Lingering traces of Song in full throttle.

Damn. That was a serious breach of Fixer protocol— Talents were supposed to stay under control. It wasn't the first time mine had leaked out from a pilot's seat, though. I looked down at my hands, remembering. Sitting on my dad's lap, barely big enough to see over the instrument panels as we flew over the barren surface of the digger rock we called home. I'd pushed buttons, banked us hard left, held on tight, and sung my three-year-old heart out.

It was one of my first memories, and one of my happiest. "I used to do that when I was a kid."

"Really?" His smile landed in his eyes first. "Janelle's mom sings to her horses, but I've never heard of anyone singing to their transpo."

Janelle was the last person I wanted to be thinking about right now. I stared out at the waving grasslands, trying to hold on to the pure, clear zing of flight.

Devan switched the ship into auto and engaged some kind of fancy shielding that blanked out the view. "Don't worry, I've set down here often enough that I could land blind, but Ophelia has great nav."

I wasn't worried. Not about the navigation, anyhow. "Why are we landing without visuals?"

"Because I'm about to show you one of BroThree's best-kept secrets, and it's better to discover it from the ground."

I'd seen the Lovatt compound off in the hazy distance before the shields had gone up—we'd essentially flown in a great big circle. "You sound like you do this a lot." The royal tour guide.

He looked over at me, vivid brown eyes no longer casual and light. "You're only the third person I've ever brought here."

I had no idea what to do with that.

He dropped the b-pod's landing gear into place and

set her down as easy as if he'd been driving a beetle. I knew enough to be impressed.

He cast me a glance. "Close your eyes."

I blinked. "What?"

He grinned. "Just do it, okay? Let me surprise you."

I gritted my teeth, closed my eyes, and let his hands navigate me out the b-pod's doors. His touch blew whatever peace I had left from Ophelia's flight to tattered shreds.

The ground under our feet softened as we walked, and the air took on a sweet, clear scent. I could hear water, but my sense of direction was totally befuddled by the lack of visuals.

"Here." Devan pulled me to a stop, his warm breath coming just over my right ear. "Welcome to one of my favorite places."

I opened my eyes and stared. I'd expected majesty—big mountains or soaring vistas. Not a quiet little meadow by a gurgling stream. Flowers danced in splashes of sunlight and mossy stumps beckoned from the shadows.

Something in my heart took a long, slow dive.

Devan pointed a finger over top of my shoulder. "I used to hang out on those branches right there and watch the water go by for hours."

I looked at the tree limbs reaching out over the water, wide and inviting and low enough for naked toes to reach the gurgles. "How did you manage to hide away for that long?" Digger-rock children weren't tracked all that closely, but I imagined that wasn't true for the son of planetary royalty.

"I jiggered the b-pod tracking." He grinned. "My parents thought I spent a lot of time holed up in my room studying."

His parents hadn't struck me as idiots. "How long did it take for you to get busted?"

"Never did." He shrugged. "Not officially, anyhow."

Someone had known—and someone had allowed a boy his hiding place, one where his feet might play in the waters of the planet he would one day rule. I scowled—I didn't want reasons to like the people who had decided that their son should be married off to smooth their planet's entry into the Federation.

My Song spurted out notes of undulating frustration, mad accompaniment to the fraying nerves under my skin.

I headed for the branches over the water. "Mind if I sit in your tree?"

"Go ahead." He was watching me carefully, a little wary. "I'll just go over here and throw pebbles."

The man didn't miss much. I felt his eyes following me as I made my way through the small brambles and weeds that grew over the base of the leaning tree. It had that slightly abandoned feeling, like it hadn't been visited as often lately.

I sang a riff of quiet comfort to the stream. Its boy had come back.

The stream returned my riff, laughing as Devan's pebbles splashed into its gurgles. I peeled off my skin boots and wiggled my naked toes. Tee's father had taught me that—touch the earth, feel the water.

I stuck my feet in, gasping a little at the cold.

Devan grinned from his spot on the riverbank. "It gets warmer later in the year."

His words barely registered. Song had risen from the stream, straight up through my toes and into the spaces between my ribs where music lived. Lush, passionate notes, and underneath them, the Song of the man at the water's edge.

Ophelia had cleared my chakras. Now the water and the man sought to fill them.

I perched, statue still, helpless to leave the swamp of personal entanglement that had threatened this mission from the first moment I'd set foot on this planet.

Devan's eyes smiled at me as a pebble dropped into the water.

I watched as he reached for another, and then I let the cold water wrap and warble around my toes—and I listened. To a stream and a man who were both agreeable on the surface, but refused to be pinned down. To a man with long practice at evading capture who had learned some of his most important lessons from this very stream. To the gratitude of the water, and of the man the boy had become. To the bond between them.

Devan Lovatt would never leave this place.

My head tipped down, protecting the sadness rising in my eyes. I let my heart rest for one long, aching moment in the certainty that he could never be mine.

And then I tumbled myself into the song of a boy who knew how to fall in love with a small river. That man was saying no to another love, and I didn't yet truly know why. The reasons people resisted were often deep and complicated and obscure. Perhaps if I swam deeper, I could see how to help.

The water gurgled at my back, guiding me. Nudging. Helping me to truly see the man.

And ran me straight into a seed so small that for a moment, I didn't recognize it for what it was.

My Song balked. I cowered, fingers digging into tree bark. I didn't want to see—and I couldn't look away.

"Hey." Devan's hand touched my arm, voice laced with concern. "You okay?"

If I had been, I wasn't now.

I gathered courage I didn't know I had and tipped my head up to meet his eyes.

The seed was there, nestled inside him. Interest and opening, kindling desire. It only needed water to grow.

Except it wasn't Janelle he turned toward. It was me.

My soul retched, wanting only to water that seed and sing to it softly of love and heartbreak. To watch its first bright-green shoots grow and to bathe them in impossible, happy light.

For one shattering moment, to let it be real.

Instead, I reached into Devan's hand, took the small black pebble in his fingers, and dropped it into the stream near my feet. I watched the ripples as it landed, watched my toes change the patterns. Listened to the minute shifts in the song of the stream that had been forever changed by my visit.

To water the seed would be a purely selfish act—and I had chosen to serve.

I sent one inaudible riff of torment into the water. A

cry for my heart—for promises I had not truly understood the weight of until now, for possibilities that would never get a chance to be.

And for what would come next, because I knew the true awfulness that lived in this moment. I had found the crack I needed, sitting in the one place I'd never thought to look—in the connection between him and me.

Singers could work with what existed. I had only to point the man my heart yearned for at someone else.

I looked at Devan one more time, aware that he was watching me with deep concern. And forced out six desolate words.

"I need to go back now."

18

I EASED my way off the landing pad, listening to the sounds of Ophelia leaving behind me. Devan had dropped me off, no questions asked—just a quiet hand on my shoulder that had nearly done me in.

I didn't have it in me to turn around and wave good-bye. All my focus was on getting my poor, bedraggled body to take one step at a time along the path to Tameka's cabin. I'd come because I couldn't face the Lovatt compound. And I'd come to do the thing I should have done the moment I laid eyes on Devan Lovatt.

"Hello there, Singer." Tameka squatted in front of a small bush near the corner of her patio. "I've got some iced tea over here, if you'd like to pour us both a glass."

My arms were working only a little better than my legs. I made my way over to the edge of the patio and sat down gingerly.

She looked at me and grinned. "How's Dusty?"

Probably laughing his ass off in a field somewhere. "Walking better than I am."

"It'll wear off in a day or two." She wielded a small pair of clippers on an errant twig. "I'm glad you got out— the grasslands seem to speak to you."

My ride with Janelle seemed the stuff of time long past. I took a deep breath. "I came to ask for your help."

She scanned me more carefully, raised an eyebrow, and said nothing.

I waited, knowing I was asking her to step across a lot of lines. Help was explicitly something our local contacts weren't supposed to hand out. And I was acutely aware that I was seeking it from the woman who had faced this same assignment once and said no.

Tameka trimmed a small sprig off the branch nearest the ground. "Is my girl giving you grief?"

I didn't like the possessives in that sentence at all. "More or less."

Her hum was one of pure satisfaction. "Figured so."

She didn't have as much figured as she thought. "She's considering the idea."

The old Dancer's eyebrows flew up in surprise. She rested her snipping tool on the ground and regarded me a long moment. "Is that your work or hers?"

That wasn't a simple question. "Both. Not anything I did, but maybe something I said."

"Words have power." Tameka's fingers moved up the branch, sure and steady—Tee's family would have hired her in a second. "And you coming here changed things before you Sang a damn note."

I hadn't Sung any good ones. "KarmaCorp will think I shifted her. I want you to tell them the truth." I owed a friend that much.

She glanced at me curiously. "If you like. They may find it difficult to believe."

"Do you?"

"No." Tameka smiled wryly. "KarmaCorp doesn't know my girl. Janelle's a woman capable of changing her own mind. It sounds like maybe she has."

I wished I could share her confidence, but the truth was, I'd never know. I leaned back against a post on her porch, my throat feeling like pulverized rock. I knew what I had to ask next, and I hated every necessary iota of it. "That isn't the help I came to ask for."

Her eyebrows raised again. "You have at least half your mission underway. Seems like you're doing pretty well."

"It's the other half that's the problem."

"Devan?" Tameka chuckled and moved her hands to a higher branch. "If Janelle's coming around, you might just leave that part up to her."

The glass shards in my gut heaved. "It won't be fast enough." I needed them pointed at each other, and I needed it now, so that I could get the hell off this planet and pull my shit back together before I did something eternally stupid.

"Ah." Tameka spoke the single syllable very quietly. "I didn't see that coming."

My eyes flew to her face, reading the surprise. The empathy. The quietly dawning fascination. And the subtle movements of her hands as she put her Talent in motion.

Verifying what she already knew.

"I know you didn't want to be the one to shift Janelle, but she's on the move now." I hated the desperate edge in my voice. "A little nudge on the Inheritor Elect and they can live happily ever after."

"Oh, I don't think so." My host had her clippers back in her hand, shearing twigs merrily. "It sounds to me like this isn't anywhere near the end just yet. Very interesting."

That was the last thing in the galaxy I wanted it to be. The nausea rose higher up my throat. "Please." I was perilously close to begging. "You've got the Talent to shift him."

Her eyebrows were damned expressive. "So do you."

I closed my eyes, took a deep breath, and told the abject, unvarnished truth. "I don't know if I can." I had found the cracks. I wasn't at all sure I could find the courage to use them.

Small, strong fingers briefly gripped mine. "Then I guess you've got a bit of a mess on your hands."

"You won't help."

"Oh, I might be very willing to help if you asked for the right kind of assistance. But I don't think this is it."

"It's what KarmaCorp ordered." And retired or not, she damn well worked for the same company I did.

"It is." A long pause as she reached for a branch at eye level and tugged it loose from its neighbors. "Sounds like your ride on Dusty jiggled quite a few things loose."

Dusty had begun the shaking. A man and his stream had finished it. "This can't be about me—I knew that before I ever got placed on field assignment. So did you."

She shrugged. "Sometimes rules and genetics butt heads. And when they do, DNA usually wins."

I'd been found on the side of a digger rock. "My DNA has pretty sketchy origins."

"You're a literalist, are you?" Her hands moved in graceful swirls, still holding the clippers. "I believe we grow our DNA, choose it. Or it chooses us. You're far more than a cog in the KarmaCorp wheel, and I suspect you've always known that."

The blonde demon child had known it. I had no idea what I knew anymore. "I got sent here to be a cog."

Tameka was silent for a moment, an odd smile on her face. "Perhaps."

I hadn't come to her cabin to get more tangled up, dammit. "What's that supposed to mean?"

She bowed her head slightly, as if acknowledging something. "As Fixers, we seek to create balance in the universe, and I've always believed that's a fine and noble calling."

So did most of us who agreed to be cogs. I Sang a trio of notes that came out mostly like a growl.

Tameka chuckled. "I'm not spouting the company line at you, or I'm not meaning to, anyhow. I believe deeply in what we do, but I think the bureaucrats and prognosticators sometimes get the details wrong."

That was heresy. "It's not my job to understand the

big picture. We get too involved to be objective." Especially this time.

"Quite often." She didn't seem all that upset by the admission. "But I've never been convinced that objectivity makes someone more right. We're human beings, and one of the things that makes us most human is the ability to put our hearts into everything we do."

"You think Talents should just get to run wild and do whatever our hearts tell us?" That was well past heresy.

"Hardly. I think we do well to have checks and balances in the system, and KarmaCorp works very hard and diligently to make that happen." She paused. "But when they convince an individual with your kind of Talent that you must only follow the rules and not listen to your own heart and your own wisdom, I believe they've made an error."

"A StarReader called this one. Not some bureaucrat in a chair." Which wasn't something she was ever supposed to know, but my control was whisper thin. She was calmly shredding everything I believed in.

"StarReaders sit in chairs too. They're fallible human beings who fart after breakfast and cry at bad movies and act entirely stupidly when they're in love, just like the rest of us."

I gaped, mouth hanging open. Those words had been said with a whole lot of personal vehemence. "It sounds like you know one." That was almost unthinkable—StarReaders lived in cloistered towers, entirely isolated from the humanity they served.

"Knew." She sighed. "An old Dancer's stories don't

matter overmuch, Singer. Be true to KarmaCorp—just know that sometimes being true to the larger mission might require bending the rules of the one they gave you."

I could feel sick confusion burning hot up my throat. I'd grown up on a digger rock, where most of life revolved around two commands. Dig and stop. Either you followed orders, or you gave them. The demon child might have rebelled against the strictures, but she deeply believed they were the way the world worked. "That sounds dangerous and complicated."

"Life is dangerous and complicated," said Tameka quietly. She set down her clippers and stood up, eyes on mine. "But I don't think that's why you came to my landing pad. How is your heart, Lakisha Drinkwater?"

Bruised in every way possible. I turned away, rejecting the concern in her voice—it was the last thing I needed to hear. "It doesn't matter."

She stepped closer. "It matters a very great deal."

"Well, I have no bloody clue."

"That would be an acceptable answer if it were true, but I don't believe it is." Her words had the ring of imperial orders.

The demon child clawed the rest of her way loose and I spun on the woman with stern eyes and muddy knees, ready to spit nails. "What the hell do you want from me?"

"I want you to find your truth."

No, she most definitely didn't. "It's pretty damn simple. I fucked up, you probably fucked up too, and one of us needs to go and face the music at headquarters." For one weak, pitiful nanosecond, I wished it could be her.

Her stern gaze didn't flicker a millimeter. "You need to face the music here first."

Fury rose, hot and white and looking for something to incinerate.

"Ah, yes," said Tameka, hands moving sharply. "That's exactly what you need to do. Let out that rage, child of the rocks, and see what lies beneath it."

The sound that came out of me was some kind of tortured, primal howl.

She tipped her head up to the sky and laughed. "Yes, that. Exactly that." She started moving, in her muddy pants and ancient boots, into a Dance far different than anything I'd ever seen. Slashing, swirling motion, feet and fists and arching spine hurling anger at the grasses, the sky, the planet, and the great, gaping vastness beyond. An old and wise woman furious at the universe for toying with people she cared about very much.

I was astonished to discover that one of them was me.

My own anger blew loose, fueled by days of hurt and anguished confusion. I hurled Song at the clear blue sky, careening notes of mad as hell. Mad at KarmaCorp for making it so hard to be a loyal cog. Mad at the StarReaders for being so mysterious, at Emelio for being so blind, and at Yesenia for sending me off on an impossible assignment. Mad at people who'd made me like them and fed me bacon, at the grasslands and burbling streams that spoke to my heart, at whatever random solar winds had crashed my birth mother into the side of some lonely astral rock, and mad at an old woman who saw way too much.

"At yourself, girl." Tameka's hoarse, rasping voice swirled out from her slicing, arrogant, infuriated Dance. "You're angry with yourself."

I didn't ask how she knew. Her Talent was so fearsome in this moment that she could likely read my mind. "I fucked up."

"Not yet, you haven't." Her entire body bent and arched, swirling under her single upstretched hand. A Dancer seeking. "Nothing that can't be fixed, anyhow."

My Song hurled a set of blindingly ugly chromatics out into the universe.

Tameka's movements slowed at my side. "Go see him."

"He's the Inheritor Elect, dammit. He has a job to do here." And mine would yank me around the galaxy until I was as old as the woman I faced. Or dead.

More hand flicks. "He's a man with a brain and a heart and the power to make his own choices. Do you really intend to take that away from him?"

The StarReaders intended it. "I'm just a cog."

"This isn't about KarmaCorp," said Tameka gently.

How could it not be? I sank down onto the edge of her porch, suddenly exhausted. "I'm here because they sent me."

"Yes." She moved her fingers in a beautiful swirl that tugged something deep inside my chest. "And you're here because you were born to make a difference on your walk in this life. Your Talent is only one of the ways you do that."

My fists banged down onto the porch. "Quit talking in damn circles."

She stopped moving and smiled. "You're more important than you think you are, and until you believe that and act from it, you're going to keep making stupid mistakes."

It was so very tempting to believe her. "Rogue Talents are dangerous." That had been drilled into us from the first day of class.

"Very." She nodded grimly. "To themselves, to those who love them, and to those who would save them."

I wondered what those terrible, sad eyes had seen.

She chased that thought away with one swift gesture. "There is a vast difference between an untrained Talent wildly throwing herself at the universe and a skilled Fixer embracing all that is possible."

Not that I could see.

"Ah, child." Tameka's voice oozed frustration and empathy and a whole bunch of things in between. "It isn't words you need, and yet here I am, yapping my mouth off." She rose on her toes, stretching up to the wide blue sky—and then she dropped into abrupt stillness. Only her fingertips moved, soft flutters floating on a river that only she could hear.

"Listen, child of the rocks," she whispered, and I didn't know whether she spoke with words or fingertips or both. The flutters moved up her arms and down her ribcage, a gentle, seductive swell moving with the heart of what mattered. Insisting that I see it. Demanding that I hear.

My Talent pulled me to my feet, called by the majesty of grass and sky and the quiet worship of a tough, old, wise woman who had walked places I didn't even know existed yet. I pitched my notes into audible range, riffing off the fluid dance of Tameka's hands.

She closed her eyes a moment, listening and utterly still. And then her hands led the rest of her body into swirling motion. Her feet ceased their rooting, letting go of the ground under her feet with bright, flying intention. And a singular message.

To Dance was her destiny. To Sing was mine.

I let my music free one more time, dizzy as it soared upward into the endless sky.

Tameka flew right at my side. I reached my energies to hers, the connection effortless. We had pitched our words against one another. Now we let our Talents blend. My notes bent and twisted, telling a story of lines that refused to be straight and the tangles they had made.

Her movements wrapped my tangles in undulating spirals and made them beautiful.

My Song quaked, backing hard away from the spirals and all that they whispered. I was lost now, falling—fury receding and vast emptiness rushing in to fill the vacuum.

And then Tameka Boon raised both hands to the sky, pulled down her clenched fists, and pummeled whatever she held straight into my gut.

Straight into the plexus chakra that knows who it is we need to be.

I gasped, my physical body thrashing for air—and felt what it was she'd pushed into the center of my soul.

Beauty. Possibility. The audacity for a nameless baby, orphaned on the side of a lonely asteroid, to dare to believe she was not just a cog in the workings of the universe—she was the pinnacle.

A call to the fiery demon child and her hurling need to make a dent in the world, to prove that the oxygen that had saved the baby was worth giving.

And a whisper to the woman that child had become, to stop rebelling against—and start rebelling for. Lakisha Drinkwater had broken rules, and she had followed them. It was time to start rewriting them. To become the kind of Fixer who might one day aspire to a shadow of the greatness of the woman who Danced before me.

I wrapped my arms around my ribs, knowing I had just been nudged by one of the finest Talents ever to walk the galaxy. And not at all sure I was brave enough to go where she pointed.

19

"AH, MS. DRINKWATER." A young staff person bustled over to me the second I set foot outside my bedroom, still yawning after a two-hour nap. "We've been looking for you—a guest has arrived to see you."

I wasn't remotely capable of dealing with company. I needed three days in seclusion, some of Tee's hot cocoa, and enough mindless vids to turn my brain to mush. "Could it perhaps wait? I've had a very busy day, and my voice needs tending." I felt pathetic as I said it, even though every word was true.

"Well." The teenager who had greeted me looked very doubtful. "Mr. Emerson might be willing, but his small companion is rather energetic."

Somewhere in the fog of my brain, I knew that name. I dug for it—trainees learned early that there was often no greater sin than failing to remember the name of some major functionary or minor noble.

A thick swirl of gray moved grudgingly aside. Ah,

when I'd boarded the cubesat to come here—the nice man who had recognized me as a Singer. I was astonished to hear he was on Bromelain III. He hadn't been on my transpo ferry, and this wasn't exactly a popular travel zone.

And he was apparently here to see me.

That roused my curiosity enough to reconsider. It would be unconscionably rude to walk off, but a moment ago, I hadn't cared. The memory of a man who had shown me both respect and kindness was enough prodding to dig out my manners. I gestured to the staffer to lead the way. "You said that Mr. Emerson has someone with him?"

"Yes."

I raised an eyebrow at the scant reply, but left it at that—I'd see for myself soon enough.

My escort led me down the cool, shadowed hallways and through enough turns that even my digger-trained internal compass started paying attention. We stopped at the door to a drawing room straight out of a fantasy novel —high double doors, red velvet curtains, and a fireplace big enough to swallow a b-pod. The teenager backed away down the hall. Evidently, I got to introduce myself.

The man I remembered turned from his spot at a window as I stepped onto the lush carpet. "Hello, Singer. It's lovely to see you again."

His eyes were as lively and intelligent as I remembered them. "I was pleased to hear you were here, Mr. Emerson. I didn't know you lived on Bromelain III." This place had a lot of very well-connected people for a back-water rock.

"Please call me Ralph. And I don't, but I visit often—I have family up north planet."

Huh. I didn't know who he was, but anyone who could travel freely between the colonies and inner planets was a very big cheese indeed. "In that case, I appreciate you interrupting your visit to come say hello."

"It seems we picked a good day to come. We're looking forward to tonight's entertainment. I enjoy these musical evenings very much, and I'm grateful to you for providing an excuse for one."

Alarm bells started ringing in my tattered brain. "I've been out all day—I wasn't aware of any entertainment this evening."

"Ah. Devan said you were the guest of honor." He smiled graciously. "The invitations went out only a few hours ago—I do hope I haven't ruined a surprise."

A few hours ago, Devan and Ophelia had dropped me off at Tameka's cabin. My stomach clenched. There was no need to shoot the accidental messenger, however. "I'm always pleased to listen to good music."

"I think you'll enjoy it." Ralph was still smiling, but his intelligent eyes were watching me carefully. "These evenings loosely follow the traditions of the Irish and Scottish of Earth, but we've made it our own."

Food, dance, and booze were pretty universal—and apparently today wasn't done trying to run me into the side of an asteroid. "I'll look forward to it. I'm glad you could make the trip." The latter, at least, was actually true. He had a very comforting energy about him.

"Not just me." Ralph inclined his head and gestured at a nearby chair. "Malia kindly accompanied me."

I stared at the empty chair, confused—and then I saw the black curls sticking out from underneath it. I crouched down to take a closer look just as two grubby hands reached up to part the curls. Bright green eyes peered out from a face that looked like it never stood still. "Hi. Granddad says you're a really important person and I should try to use my best manners, but it's okay if I forget sometimes."

I grinned at the imp with streaks of dirt on her face, knowing a kindred spirit when I saw one. "I forget sometimes too."

"This," said Ralph, crouching down to join us, "is my youngest granddaughter, Malia. She likes to fly, so I brought her along to keep me company."

Malia scowled. "Momma says you're always supposed to tell the truth, Granddad. This lady is one of those Fixer people, just like Auntie Bri, and you want her to check me for Talent." She flashed a grin at me. "I'm a really good singer."

He reached over and tweaked her nose. "And a cheeky ruffian, aren't you?"

Her head tilted sideways. "I don't know. What's a ruffian?"

He smiled. "A very good word to look up on the GooglePlex."

She grinned over at me, rolling her eyes as she

crawled out from under the chair. "That's what he always says."

She was taller than I expected, all gangly limbs and wild black curls. And after my day thus far, cheeky balm for my ragged soul. "How old are you, sweetie?"

"Seven." She plopped down on the carpet, since Ralph and I hadn't made it to our feet yet. "Do you want to hear me sing?"

It was rare for Fixers to test for Talent in the field—we were generally trying to keep a low profile, and the Seekers didn't tend to appreciate us milling around on their turf. I glanced over at Ralph. "Has she been tested before?" With Fixers in the family, someone had probably done a quiet check.

"Not for several years." He ruffled Malia's hair. "She was born singing, so we've kept a watch on her. Bri's Talent isn't strong enough to sense resonance, but she brought a friend for a visit about three years back—a Dancer by the name of Yalonda Keyes."

I knew Yalonda—she was more than strong enough to feel the vibrations of an emerging Talent. "What did she tell you?"

He kept his eyes calm and noncommittal. "She said to keep watching her."

That could mean almost anything.

Malia squiggled forward on the rug. "Is it fun to be a Singer?"

This was a bad day to ask. "Sometimes. Mostly it's hard work."

"I'm a pretty good worker." Her eyes sparkled. "Do you get to visit lots of planets like Auntie Bri?"

I'd fantasized about space travel as a kid too. The cramped insides of an econo cubesat had been a rude awakening. I needed to be careful, however—if the kid had Talent, KarmaCorp wasn't going to much care what her personal travel wishes were. Talents were too precious, and untrained Talents too dangerous, to worry about little issues like individual choice.

I sighed. Tameka might have crawled under my skin, but KarmaCorp was far from evil, and the job wasn't nearly that black and white. Fixers had a wide range of work they could choose to do, and most of us found a niche that made us happy enough. And from what I'd seen of the rest of the world, driving your own life wasn't necessarily all it was cracked up to be. Some people are pretty intent on screwing up no matter what, and some bloom where they're planted, even if the soil sucks.

"You sound tired." Malia's forehead had creased in wrinkles.

Damn, I'd totally blanked on answering her question. "I am—it's been a long day."

She nodded sagely, like she understood the strange adult concept of running out of energy. "Maybe I can sing you a lullaby—Momma says that helps sometimes."

That was interesting. "Is your mom tired a lot?"

"Only when Henrique and Tao are being brats." She grinned. "They'd exhaust anybody."

Ralph chuckled quietly. "Malia's twin brothers. They're two."

Tee's sister had twins, and after a couple of hours childminding them once, I'd been ready to die. "Do you sing to your brothers?"

"Nope. Momma says they'll sleep when they're good and ready, and the rest of us just have to buck up. I help play with them, though. They like the game where we jump on the gel-couches and try not to touch the poisonous swamp on the floor."

I remembered a version of that one, although digger rocks didn't tend to run to swank decor like gel-couches. "How many of you has the swamp managed to eat?"

Malia giggled. "It got Granddad's toes once."

"Did not." Ralph sounded insulted at the mere suggestion. "It only licked them."

The kid rolled her eyes again, lips tightly closed, and gave him a look that promised the conversation wasn't nearly over. One seven-year-old, trying to remember her best manners.

I watched the light dancing in both their eyes and tried not to be envious. It sounded like a normal, happy childhood—the kind most people never even caught glimpse of. She was a really lucky kid. "Got any songs about the swamp monsters?" Kids with Talent usually had an oversized love of the dramatic, and it would help magnify whatever resonance she might have.

She shook her head. "No, but I bet I could make one up."

She probably could, but I wasn't sure I had the energy. And there were easier ways, albeit less fun ones.

"How about I Sing a few notes, and you sing along with me—whatever wants to come out?"

"Okay." She sat up a little straighter and pulled air into her flexible lungs. "Can Granddad sing too? He does musical theater, and he has a really nice voice."

I looked at Ralph and shrugged. "Sure." Whatever made the kid feel more comfortable.

He smiled at his granddaughter and mimicked her good posture.

I let a couple of breaths massage my ribs, and then I started in my high midrange, sounding some basic tones. Malia listened for a few notes and started chiming in with ones of her own. She had a sweet, clear voice and a natural sense of harmony. I focused on her energy resonances as Ralph added chord intervals below us.

My Song didn't sense Talent from either of them.

I shifted, moving lower in my range. Digging. Sometimes miners went deep on pure instinct.

Malia followed me down, picking out pretty intervals, adding a few interesting shifts, and frowning harder the lower we got. I waited, swimming around a basic chord progression, wondering what she would do.

She tailed me for a couple of spins and then she inhaled, eyes sparkling, and flew up a steep run to an octave most singers could only dream of. I followed her up, hearing my larynx gurgling in protest. It was a range I could sing in, but just barely—and I usually babied my vocal chords a whole lot on the way there.

Malia rippled through the high notes like a butterfly, light and sure with flashes of glorious color. I took a moment to appreciate the pure, incandescent beauty of her voice. I knew good singing, and hers was glorious. There were a hundred inner-planet opera houses that would line up for a chance to train her.

They'd never get the chance. In this range, the kid had Talent streaming from every cell.

I glanced at Ralph, saw his gentle smile, and nodded, confirming what he already knew. And was fiercely glad to see the protective instincts rising in his eyes. Good. KarmaCorp would come for Malia in three years. In the meantime, she'd be in very good hands.

Talent like hers was a highly desirable commodity, and grabbing young girls before the Seekers found them was extremely profitable business, even with half the Federation on their tails. And then there were the garden-variety corrupters—the people who thought just a small nudge couldn't hurt, a little tweaking of the universe on their behalf.

If the look in Ralph's eyes was any indication, swamp monsters would be the worst thing Malia had to worry about.

She'd stopped singing and sat watching me, still as a statue.

Hoping. Wishing. Wanting the answer to be yes.

That had never been me—I'd hated every minute of discovering I had Talent and what it meant. It was humbling to see her want, so clearly, to step into the shoes I wore. I reached for my subsonics and sent a gentle, welcoming trill her direction.

Joy streaked across her face, and a response came

back—excited, effervescent, and insanely loud in the frequencies only I could hear.

I laughed. "You need a little work on your volume control, kiddo." Especially if she had subsonics at seven years old.

"How did you do that?" She practically bounced herself into my lap. "That thing I could feel inside my brain, how did you do that?"

I'd been doing it for a lot longer than she'd been alive, and I still didn't really have any idea. "That's what they'll teach you on Stardust Prime." In the meantime, she'd just deafen the odd pig or bird.

She'd bounced over to Ralph's lap now. "I'm going to be a Fixer!"

"I know, brightness." He stroked the back of her hair. "I believe you'll make a very fine one."

She turned toward me, eyes shining like the noonday sun. "Granddad says it's really important work, helping the universe to have good balance."

He'd been preparing her, then. "I think so." I soaked in her innocent, steadfast belief that what I did mattered.

Ralph was still stroking her hair. "We live in a galaxy more peaceful, more just, more rich in beauty and diversity and freedom than anything that has ever come before us, thanks to the hard work of Lakisha and the other people at KarmaCorp."

His belief wasn't so innocent, but it was just as steadfast. I felt my battered soul drinking it in. Tameka Boon was only one voice—there were others.

Malia smiled up at him. "We live in a good world. We're really lucky."

"We are—and you're going to help keep us that way."

She nodded and looked over at me. "Do lots of things lose their balance? My brothers used to fall down a lot, and it made them cry."

The universe didn't bounce nearly as well as most toddlers. "We try to help catch things before they land on the ground." It was a lot easier than trying to put galactic Humpty Dumpties back together.

She frowned. "That sounds hard."

Someday, she would walk in my shoes and feel the hard for herself. But not today. "KarmaCorp has lots of really smart people who help us know what to do."

She nodded, a child who still trusted the advisers in her world to be sane and good and right. And a child who would one day be a mighty tool for those trying to act on the side of good in the universe.

Just like I was. I bowed my head, acknowledging the crooked lines and the message I'd just been sent.

Destiny wasn't mine to make—it was mine to work in service of. Rebel demon child I might be, but I wanted to be proud of myself when I woke up and looked in the mirror. Or when I looked into the eyes of seven-year-olds who someday wanted to be me.

I was here to help sway two good people toward serving the highest good. A whole pile of KarmaCorp bigwigs would have blessed this mission before I got assigned to it, and I had no more business questioning it than Malia did. I was a Singer, not an Anthro or a Star-

Reader or a boss lady. It wasn't my job to understand the importance or rightness of the assignment I'd been given —it was just my job to do it. To trust that I was making a difference that mattered.

Even if it made my heart scream.

20

ALWAYS GO OUT WITH A BANG. I'd grown up in a place that took that sentiment pretty literally, but I figured it applied elsewhere too.

I'd run my mission here into a mountain of rock more times than I could count, but I was done hiding in shadows. Which was good, because the ballroom sprawled out below me was dazzlingly well lit. Glow bulbs and firefly lights floated above food-laden tables and a dance floor that looked to be filled with half the population of Bromelain III.

"Well hello, Singer."

I turned and spied the owner of the voice behind me, lounging against a wall. "Shouldn't you be down there dancing?"

"There will be time." Tameka regarded my outfit and raised a wry eyebrow. "If you think that's going to dissuade Devan Lovatt and do your work for you, you've seriously misjudged him."

I hadn't dressed for him. I'd dressed for me. Lace-up miner boots, black leather fingerless gloves, and a short, tight dress crisscrossed in synth-leather and grommets and not much else. Hair in a braid that would have screamed "looking for a fight" in any bar on any mining asteroid in the galaxy, and around my neck, the gold retro headphones that traveled with me everywhere and normally never saw the light of day.

Digger-chick regalia to the max, and badass, every inch. Not remotely appropriate attire for this event, and I didn't care. I needed to do what KarmaCorp had sent me to do—but I could darn well do it Lakisha Drinkwater style. "I wasn't aware there was a dress code."

"There isn't." The old Fixer's lips quirked. "Feeling prickly, are you?"

Apparently. I touched my hands to the headphones around my neck. They were the first thing I'd bought with the first Commonwealth credits I'd ever made. I'd been sixteen and dumb, and I still adored the hell out of them.

Tameka was watching my hands and smiling softly. "My grandmother used to own a pair of those."

I had zero interest in making small talk, but I also had an annoying fondness for the old woman trying to engage me in it. "She was a Singer?"

"No. A generator mechanic. Said they were the best ear protection out there."

There were a bunch of drill operators I knew who agreed with her.

She stepped away from the wall. "Go, girl. Make your impression." Her smile was full of mystery this time. "And do yourself a favor."

She was the last person on earth I wanted advice from in this moment. "And what would that be?"

"Listen to the impression you actually make."

I gave her a glare that even I knew seriously lacked in maturity, and then headed down the long, sweeping staircase into the ballroom. Every step I took drummed in the fact that miner boots weren't the normal footwear gracing these treads. Judging from what I could see below, attire here ran to fancy, sparkly, and dainty as hell.

Good. It was time we all remembered I didn't belong here.

"Singer." If the man who normally handled affairs in the Lovatts' breakfast room was at all surprised by my appearance, he hid it well. "The Inheritor Elect bids you welcome."

I didn't stop to talk—especially about the Inheritor Elect. Whatever Devan's plans might be for this evening of his, I was here to work. I made my way through the ballroom, Fixer antennae on high alert. Brushing the edges of gatherings, reading, analyzing. Looking for any last leverage to do the job I'd been sent to do.

Always go out with a bang.

By the time I'd reached the other side of the ballroom, my bang had turned into a whimper. No signs of leverage —and I'd misjudged the entire damn planet. Half the people here had interrupted their night to say hello, and the commentary on my outfit had been complimentary to the last word.

A planet of individualists, attracted to one who had dared to be individual. Not remotely what I'd intended, and not the ideal vibe for a woman who'd come here to finally be a decent cog, but it was too freaking late to go change. And it probably wasn't all that reasonable to be mad at a whole colony for being friendly. I clomped in my miner boots, clutched my headphones, damned Tameka for being right, and made do.

"You look ready to chew nails."

I scowled at Janelle, gliding along a sparkling gold rug my direction. "I'm hungry, that's all."

She looped a silk-clad hand through my elbow. "Food's this way."

I looked at our conjoined arms and tried not to be amused. "That's quite the outfit." Hers flowed from a snug blue sleeveless top down into layers of shimmering, almost translucent floor-length skirt. A far cry from the woman on horseback. Intergalactic royalty hanging out with the digger-rock brat.

She followed my gaze. "What, you don't like blue?"

It was gorgeous, and if it were mine, I'd probably never take it off. I sighed and let some of my cranky go. "It's really pretty—it's just not what I expected to see you wearing."

"I could say the same." She grinned and looked down. "I'm totally stealing those boots the next time you're not looking."

It so wasn't the night for friendship to be sneaking in

my cracks—and yet I had no idea how to resist. "They're the height of miner fashion." And she could have traded her dress for about a million pairs of them.

She tugged us sideways into a break in the traffic around one of the immensely loaded food tables. "Chocolate first, or real food?"

Chocolate was real food. However, I'd spied something far harder to get on Stardust Prime. "Bacon, then chocolate."

The sound that came out of Janelle was almost a giggle. "I think you're an addict."

"Guilty." And determined to indulge the only one of my cravings that seemed safe.

"Here." She handed me two bowls and reached a ladle toward a pot of beautiful hammered copper. "These are baked apples. We'll put some of the bacon on these, and some of the cheese from that plate over there, and then we'll go hide so nobody steals our bounty."

I stood still and acted as a serving tray while she filled two bowls with steaming apples. They smelled like butter and cinnamon, and it was all I could do not to plop myself in face first.

This planet knew how to throw a punch.

Janelle peeled off her gloves and reached for two long slices of bacon, crumbling them on top of the apples. It didn't dim the sense of galactic royalty at all.

"You'll want cheese on that," said a woman I didn't know, dressed in a flowing sheath of gold and purple and holding out a plate mounded high in bright yellow shredded stuff.

"Thanks, Auntie D." Janelle swooped down on the cheese and dropped a kiss on the cheek of its bearer. "It's yours, yes?"

"Straight out of the curing cave this morning."

Janelle added huge handfuls to the top of each of the bowls I held. My stomach let loose a growl loud enough to be heard in the next quadrant.

Auntie D laughed and set the cheese plate down again. "You both look lovely tonight. It's nice to see you enjoying your evening, Singer."

I blinked, shocked to discover that in this moment, I actually was. "Thank you. And apparently, my stomach thanks you too. The cheese smells wonderful." Tee's family made cheese for very special occasions, but it was soft and fresh. This had a tang that reminded me oddly of rocks, in the best possible way.

She chuckled and dropped a spoon in each bowl. "It tastes even better. Go eat, before the masses realize they're hungry."

Janelle grinned and motioned with her head, leading me off to a spot in the shadows. I followed, suddenly grateful for a moment to hide.

She took one of the bowls from my hand and toasted me with it. "Food of the gods."

I picked up my spoon, appropriately reverent and suddenly starving—and had to struggle to keep my knees from buckling as I slid in the first bite and nearly drowned in cinnamon-buttered, bacon-topped bliss.

Janelle laughed at my appreciative hum and talked

around her own mouthful. "My sister says it's better than sex."

Her sister was right, and I'd had some pretty good sex.

A hand reached around me and tugged on Janelle's hair. "You obviously need to pick better partners."

I turned, nerves totally shot—and nearly landed my apples in Devan's chest.

He was dressed in midnight-blue silk and leather that should have looked as ridiculous as my outfit—and gave him the vibe of a wandering galactic bard instead.

A really sexy bard. My nose yearned to cross the final inches and bury itself in blue silk and the smell of him.

I was losing this bar fight. Badly.

He backed up half a step and looked at me carefully. "Hello." One word, his eyes saying dozens more.

I couldn't deal with any of them. "I'm probably supposed to thank you for putting on this shindig in my honor."

Janelle swallowed a choking laugh beside me.

Amusement joined whatever else Devan's eyes were saying. "Probably."

No one got to laugh at me tonight, especially these two. "I don't like being manipulated." Especially when I had no idea what he was up to.

"That's an interesting statement from a Fixer." Steel now, and not a small dose of it.

Every digger-rock cell I possessed fired up. And then froze as Devan got wrapped in purple-and-gold exuberance.

"There's my beautiful boy." The woman I knew only as Auntie D kissed Devan thoroughly and patted his cheek. "You've been hiding—I haven't been able to find you all night." She reached into her copious bag and pulled out a thick, round package. "I brought some of your favorite."

His eyes softened. "Thank you. Nobody makes cheese like you do."

"Of course they don't." She patted his cheek, delighted. "Let's go put it into your cellar. You know it doesn't like to be out of a nice chill, and it's been in my bag for hours now."

Janelle's choking laugh had started up again.

I watched, bemused and still sparking, as the man who would one day rule this planet sent me a rueful, laden glance and walked off to help a woman who clearly adored him—and thought he was five—tuck away a round of cheese. I could hardly stand the lump in my heart.

"Well." Janelle cleared her throat beside me. "That was interesting."

I shoveled in a huge spoonful of warm apples. They tasted like sawdust.

"Kish." Her voice was as gentle as I'd ever heard it.

"He's meant to be yours." My words sounded like they came from someplace very far away.

"Like hell he is."

I could feel the window for me to complete my mission clanging shut. "It could work. You like him."

"Not really."

The warm apples in my belly rolled over hard, and I

just wanted to scream. "Don't freaking lie to a Singer—it doesn't work."

"I'm not lying." Her eyes flashed blue fire. "I'd started sniffing around that gate, don't get me wrong. But I don't walk through every gate I sniff at, and I don't need to walk through this one." She paused a beat, her gaze never wavering. "I think you do."

Her words were a fist to my already battered gut.

Janelle gave a disgusted grunt and steered us into a quiet corner. "If I wasn't such an idiot, I'd have figured it out a lot sooner."

"You would *not* have." I might have blown the hell out of this assignment, but I knew how to keep my damn feelings under wraps.

She looked at me again, and her eyes softened. "It's written all over your face, Kish."

I closed my eyes, utterly naked and defeated. "I'm so sorry."

"Why?"

Her obvious confusion yanked my eyes back open. "Because it's impossible. Because he's supposed to be yours. Because I came here with a job to do and I'm not sure I could have blown it more ways if I tried."

She shrugged. "So you screwed up. Life goes on."

It wasn't nearly that simple. "The things we get sent to do matter. They're like the butterfly wings that flap and make a thunderstorm calm down on the other side of the quadrant." Little levers to do big work.

Janelle chuckled. "Do all Fixers have such big egos?"

I wasn't sure whether to be insulted or infuriated that

she still wasn't getting it. "*We're* not important, but what we *do* is."

"Fine. You work for a company that has a big ego," she said wryly. "I get that you folks in the inner planets take all that stuff pretty seriously, but out here we know that life happens and it doesn't always go the way you planned."

I didn't punch her nose. Barely. "Did you just call me a dumb flatlander?"

She raised a sharp eyebrow. "Do I need to? You like a guy. Since when is that reason to act like an idiot and stand here spouting stupid lines about the fate of the galaxy?"

I bowed my head, KarmaCorp ideals at serious war with the siren song my heart wanted so badly to believe. "Neither of us know what will happen if you and Devan don't connect. There could be ripples all over the universe." StarReaders didn't get involved otherwise.

She shrugged. "We won't die if the Federation rejects us, and everyone on Bromelain III can take care of themselves. It's not my job to keep the whole damn ocean smooth."

I felt the weight, so heavy I could barely breathe. "That pretty much *is* my job."

"Bleeding hell." She reached out and grabbed my hand. "I refuse to let any friend of mine sound like a flatlander with a really swollen head. Come on."

I planted my feet as well as two miner boots could plant. "I'm not going anywhere."

"Yes, you are." Her eyes were flashing blue fire again

as she gave my arm a good tug. "We're going to solve this problem the smart way."

I looked at her fisted right hand, prepared to be surprised one more time. "And how would that be, exactly?"

She grinned. "With chocolate."

I could have resisted the fire and the orders, the threats and general bossiness. But even digger boots can't fight friendship and chocolate.

-ooo-

"I don't think I'm going to be able to move from this spot for a week." My stomach was stretched in ways I hadn't known it was capable of. Janelle and I had dealt with the boggy ground of Devan Lovatt and man troubles the age-old way—we'd thrown buckets of food at it.

Janelle, lounging on a chair beside me, opened her mouth to answer—and then abruptly shifted, her face letting go of mellow and sliding back into the woman who rode the grasslands on a horse and had very few doubts.

I turned on my chair and ended up eye to eye with Ralph Emerson's bowl—it was almost as big as his head.

"Good evening, Singer." He turned slightly to address my companion. "And to the lovely Mistress Brooker."

She nodded, a friendly smile in place and genuine warmth in her tone. "Ralph. It's good to see you again. Did you bring any of your imps along?"

He grinned. "Just one—Malia is with me this time."

"Ah."

A world of meaning packed into one syllable. I watched silently, fascinated by the ripples as two parts of my temporary world collided. Tameka had hinted that there were other sources of power here on Bromelain III. Judging from what I saw in front of me, some of them had the name Emerson attached.

However, once again, all parties involved seemed pretty thoroughly mired in mutual respect. Whatever the Anthro models said, I just couldn't see this planet imploding. Too many stable, capable, independent types.

Ralph turned as the noise from the crowd behind him dimmed considerably. "I believe the evening's entertainment is about to get underway."

Somehow, in my bacon-and-apple stupor, I'd managed to forget why we were here. I followed his gaze, trepidation rising.

Evgenia Lovatt had stepped into a bright spotlight on the ethereal, starry stage, a state-of-the-art acoustic microphone in her hand. "Good evening, everyone. Thank you for coming on such short notice to help us share our love of music and song with our honored guest." She gestured my direction, clearly well aware of which shadows I inhabited. "We have a KarmaCorp Singer in our midst, as I'm sure you've all heard, come to assist us with our bid to join the Federation."

That was an audacious spin. Light murmuring in the audience seemed to suggest that I wasn't the only one who had noticed. KarmaCorp didn't align itself with political interests, especially those of a minor outpost colony. Evgenia might have named the reason I'd been requested, but it was highly unlikely that it was the reason I'd been sent. The StarReaders had seen something else—something that mattered enough to have landed in an Ears Only file. I would likely never know what, and neither would anyone in this ballroom.

Unlike them, I had to believe it was something that mattered.

I slid off my chair and stepped out of the shadows—Fixers normally hid in dark corners just fine, but my digger-chick instincts didn't think that was the answer right now.

"Normally, we let our honored guests sit quietly." Evgenia paused and looked around the ballroom, gauging interest. Holding attention. "But I have it on good authority that we have a lovely new voice in our midst, and I was hoping she could be persuaded to share a song or two." She held out a hand in my direction. "Singer, if you would be so kind as to indulge us?"

I stood pinned to the ground, stupefied. I was a KarmaCorp Fixer, not an entertainer.

Ralph chuckled quietly behind me. "What did you do to get under her skin?"

It wasn't Evgenia I was concerned about—whatever the glint in her eyes might be saying, she wasn't the architect of this evening. "I don't sing in public."

"That's one possible answer." His voice was full of wry amusement. "Perhaps not the most politically expedient one, however."

Cart him to hell and back for being right. I'd created

enough of a mess on Bromelain III without refusing a direct and very public request from the royal matriarch, even if she was engaging in the body-slam version of diplomatic dancing. Or her son was. I swallowed a goodly chunk of digger-rock attitude and tried to sort out an answer that would keep the imprint of Yesenia Mayes' boots off my behind.

Janelle had stepped up beside me, lips quirking, but saying nothing. A friend who let her friends fight their own battles—or fed them happily enough to a certain wolf.

I fingered my gold headphones, thinking fast. And then I found my tunnel entrance and looked back at Ralph Emerson. "Do you happen to know where Malia is?"

His eyebrows shot up a little. "Yes."

I grinned and let the chick from the digger rock loose. "Good. Grab her and meet me at the microphone, will you? The three of us sounded pretty good together earlier."

His eyebrows shot up a whole lot farther—and then his eyes filled with amused respect. "Indeed we did."

I spun on the heel of my miner boots and headed for the stage. One fight, or whatever the hell this was, engaged. I hoped the man who had started it was paying attention.

Evgenia watched my approach and handed over the microphone without comment. I ignored her utterly and turned to face the audience. "Hello, everyone. This isn't usually part of my job description, so I've asked a couple of the people here tonight to help me out."

The audience started craning their necks to see. Beside me, Evgenia's spine got noticeably more rigid. I kept ignoring her, pretty sure she was no match for Malia Emerson.

Ralph arrived at the edge of the stage first and stepped back to let his granddaughter ascend the stairs ahead of him. Murmurs started in the crowd—clearly at least some of the attendees knew who she was. I flashed her a grin and then crouched down as she arrived at my side, covering the mike. "Will you sing with me exactly like we did this afternoon?" I glanced over at the man just arriving. "Your granddad can take the lead this time, and we'll both play with the melody he's singing."

"No pressure," said Ralph dryly.

I wasn't worried—I'd heard him sing. "Stage fright?"

He chuckled. "No."

I handed him the microphone. Malia and I wouldn't need one—Talent would magnify whatever vocal chords couldn't. He cleared his throat and looked out at the hushed crowd. "For those of you who don't know me, I'm Ralph Emerson, and you likely know my family from over north way. I'll be the guy holding the coats while these two lovely ladies wow you with their voices."

People laughed, and the watchful energy subsided. Ralph, taking the pressure off all of us with an ease that suggested long experience in front of fractious crowds. He looked down at his granddaughter and winked. "If I sing off key, kick my ankles gently, okay?"

Malia grinned. "Kicking's not nice manners."

The audience laughed, and those who seemed to know the child laughed loudest.

My nonexistent entertainer skills were nicely being made redundant.

Ralph nodded at me and picked up a melody line that I quickly recognized as the one Malia and I had been playing with at the end of her testing. I was impressed—he had it nailed, right down to the trills and tricky harmonics.

His granddaughter, not shy at all, was already joining in with some high overnotes. Not a lot of volume yet, and she hadn't let her Talent loose.

I listened to the two of them, enjoying the interplay—and then I remembered that she was an untrained seven-year-old and got my shit together. Somebody needed to drive this bus. I layered in carefully underneath her high descant. Supporting the audible tones, and encouraging her subsonics into gear.

She looked over at me and grinned as her heaping Talent came out to play.

I put up a wave perimeter to hold us steady and tried not to laugh. It was like trying to contain an overly eager puppy—I was getting my metaphorical face licked. Malia's first-year trainers were going to have their hands full.

The kid soared up an octave and then swooped down again, puppy in full flight.

The acoustics were incredibly good. This ballroom might look like a fancy dance hall, but there was no way voices sounded this good in here by accident. Someone had designed this place to be sung in.

Ralph and Malia had found their groove now, young and old singing a beautiful duet sandwich around my quiet harmonies in the middle.

Once upon a time, I'd have wanted to be the flash. Tonight, it was perfectly fine to be the most boring person on the stage. I set my hands on the headphones around my neck and sang backup to a seven-year-old and her granddad.

And then Ralph smiled, took a couple of steps back, and stopped singing.

Malia and I both turned to look at him, confused.

He gestured at the two of us, palms up.

I sent him the nastiest glare I dared with a spotlight shining on our faces. Troublemaker.

The look he sent me back was utterly bland.

His granddaughter grinned, turned back toward the audience, and slid her voice up a run that should have had glass breaking except for the sure, sheer beauty of her notes. Not an exuberant puppy anymore. Stardust and auditory magic.

I did my job and swept up behind her, the steady wind under soaring wings that didn't yet know what it was to need landing gear.

When we finished, the audience erupted. I took two steps back to stand beside Ralph and let a gangly girl with shining eyes take her bows. I needed a moment to gather the pieces of my soul back from the heavens.

This afternoon, Malia had reminded me of why I worked. Tonight, she reminded me of why I Sang.

A slender man with dancing eyes walked up the steps and took the microphone, ruffling Malia's hair. "You're a hard act to follow, kiddo."

She laughed and blew him a kiss. "Are you going to sing the one about the silly cow who jumped over the moon?"

"Maybe. You going to sing with me?"

She shook her head earnestly. "Not this time—I need to go eat. My tummy is rumbly."

We walked off the stage to the opening bars of a nursery-rhyme medley that was clever, irreverent, and clearly well known to the listening crowd. The musicians in the corner were getting in on the action, adding their sounds as harmony, counterpoint, and the occasional barnyard animal.

I turned to listen, oddly captivated.

By the time the fifth or sixth person got up to sing, the trend was clear. The range of genres was vast—some goofy, some serious, some folk songs and some tending toward the operatic. But every last person who got up behind the mike had a good handle on how to work notes with their voice. And judging from the loose line forming stage left, there were a whole lot more very competent singers to come.

I stopped trying to analyze anything.

My headphones and I had landed in a nice spot in the standing throngs just left of center stage. I stomped my boots to the beat when there was one, shimmied my hips when there wasn't, and let myself sink into the joy of really good music. I had no idea why there was this depth and breadth of skilled voices on a backwater planet, why it had taken me a week to find out, or why Devan Lovatt had suddenly called them forth.

But it was apples and bacon for my soul.

21

MIDNIGHT. So the matriarch of the evening had announced, right before the last singer ascended to the stage.

The man behind the microphone kept his hands still on the eight-stringed instrument that looked like a second cousin to a guitar, and sang the opening notes a cappella. Quiet, haunting, and glorious.

I sighed, my heart stuffed full of music and all the things it called up in me. I wasn't surprised by the skill anymore. Someone on BroThree gave damn fine singing lessons—and Devan Lovatt had absolutely been a student. He had a gorgeous voice, the kind that spoke of dedicated training beneath the carefree ease. He landed like melted butter on the notes, bending them with a grace that took a well-trained diaphragm, a good ear, and some serious practice.

More importantly for this night, however, he clearly knew how to play an audience. They'd hushed the moment he'd begun to sing, and now, as he tugged at them with the tight runs that headed into the body of the old ballad, they started to lean in. All eyes on the bard.

Singing to them all. Singing only to me.

Calling to my jagged heart. Sending beauty and light into the awful, empty space between what I had to do and what I wanted.

It was a song I knew. An old folk tune, renditions of which existed all over the galaxy. One of those songs that sounded simple, and could be sung that way. Devan wasn't singing the simple version. His voice added hints of what, on another night, might be the flute or lute or electric guitar, the subtle embellishments that make a simple melody lush and poetic and captivating. His fingers added soft accompaniment on the strings.

Singing to them all. Singing only to me.

I cursed my Song as it started to hum the undertones that would mesh with man and instrument. I wasn't Devan Lovatt's backup.

His eyes found me—and asked me to be something entirely different. A man who had found the seed inside himself. A man trying to figure out what to do with it and what it meant.

My Talent oozed partway out some tiny crack in my Fixer armor. Begging. For just one song, I needed to be with him, even if no one else would ever hear it.

And then I saw Malia, two rows ahead and turned to face me, eyes glued to mine. Feeling the disturbances in the force.

Someone else would always hear.

So I kept my Talent bound and chained, and listened instead. Reached, heart yearning and soul cracking, to gather up a picture. Something to carry away when I had to go.

Devan leaned into the lines of the chorus now, a story of love and loss and the fires of home that tightened my throat, blurred my eyes, and squeezed my lungs until oxygen was a long-lost memory.

And still I listened, drinking in every last note. I would not Sing—but I would hear his Song.

It began with the same story I'd heard at his stream, one of a boy and the planet he loved, of the waters and grasses that had kept him a healthy child and grown him into a rooted and steady man. But this time, I let myself listen to the rest. The quiet notes of discontent, rising up underneath the main melody line. Not much—the remnants of teenage rebellion against the ties that bound him. A substantial dose of humor, a man who could look at most anything in his life and see the lopsided bits. A man who knew not to take himself too seriously.

I sighed. Even now, I was avoiding.

I breathed once again into the adult, responsible life I had chosen—and then I held my head high, locked my eyes with his, and let myself open to the notes that would hurt most. The music of the embryonic seed of future love, planted in the rich soils of his vibrant soul.

The one he had found and was beginning to water.

My heart soaked in the singing of the seed and the man, drinking deeply of the promise that lived there—the hope and the achingly fragile thread of what might be.

I reached for the not-so-tiny seed, every cell of my body vibrating. I would not Sing to it. Couldn't. But just for a moment, I held it and treasured what it was.

And in the most tucked-away DNA of that seed, I heard something I hadn't known. Deep inside Devan Lovatt, something hurt—and something healed.

My Talent yanked its way out of prison, seeking. Needing to know. I reached—for the scars, and for the unfurling shoots rooted in rich, deep soil that seed could become. For one, aching heartbeat, I touched the pure, glorious young green of the new leaves and their song of opening, their story of why he hadn't opened to love before. A wound so carefully and expertly disguised, I hadn't been able to see it.

My mission wasn't to Sing two stubborn hearts toward each other. It was to *open* them. It had taken only the words of a friend to encourage Janelle to dream a little. But Devan needed something different—and I had needed to see this deep into his heart to know what it was.

He was a man who had grown up in a world full of enormous gravitational forces. His parents, the Inheritor model of governance that had begun shaping his destiny well before he was born, a planet full of people who expected him to lead them one day and to earn the right to do it.

He'd survived by slithering loose. By dangling his toes in a stream where no molecule of water could ever be pinned down for more than an instant. By flying a ship tuned to escape gravity with the lightest touch of his hands. By singing to an audience, but never singing to just one.

By loving wide, but never deep.

I looked into the eyes of the man still standing alone on a stage at midnight and singing—and understood. Janelle would never have let him love her just a little, and he would have always known that. Me, I'd taken him by surprise. And because I had, that door in his heart—the one that could let in monumental, gravitational-force-sized love—had opened, just a crack.

He had opened it for me.

My Song swirled in my throat, clogging with the aching, terrible beauty of what I had to do next. I could feel the greater good. Not KarmaCorp's good, not my good. The calling of karmic rightness. The world would be immeasurably better with a Devan Lovatt in it who was open to loving deeply.

He had opened that door for me. Now I needed to ask him to keep it open—even though I would never walk through it.

My mission wasn't to get him to say yes. It was for me to say no, and to do it with enough clarity and grace that a part of Devan which he'd put away long ago could finally get the oxygen it needed to come to life.

He would do it for himself eventually—I could believe no less of the amazing man he was. But I could help it happen now. And I would do it with all the fierce love and dignity that a demon child from a digger rock could give. It would be a gift, my first and last, to a man I would never forget.

Because he was not the only one opening this night.

I called up all the skill that was mine to possess, shaping the notes in my head and my ribs, the ones that would ask his heart to stay open. I could feel my chakras snapping into alignment.

This would work. He would listen because I was the best damn Singer in this quadrant. And he would listen because the notes were mine.

I didn't bother with discretion or nuance or any semblance of the normal careful silencers a Singer used in her work. I hadn't landed on Bromelain III quietly, and it seemed I wasn't going to leave that way either. Every person here tonight would know what I did.

But only one would know why.

I let my notes go, audible range and subsonic both, a cacophony of power and sound, heat and pleading and shattering softness.

I saw Devan's jaw drop in abject shock as the first vibrations hit.

I let the shattering softness land first—I would do this as gently as I could. For a few shimmering notes, I stood in the open doorway of the heart of the man I loved and helped him heal.

And then I gathered the notes that would hold it open while I walked away.

On stage, the man of pebble and stream and laughing flight took one step toward me. And another.

My soul keened—but I didn't have much longer. I gathered every shred of courage and conviction I had left and pushed it at the man I had to leave.

And felt the wild, fierce blast of another Talent land-ing, locking my Song up tight and shielding the hell out if its intended target. I spun around, shocked to the core. Fixers didn't fight each other. Ever.

Tameka stood behind me, her silk robes spread, bare feet planted, toes curling into the floor.

I gathered up the concentration she'd demolished, reaching for the fraying echoes of my Song for Devan.

"No, child." The old Dancer held the notes out of my reach with a mere flick of her wrists. "That's not the way."

Like hell it wasn't. "It's the only way."

"Find another choice." She was having to work harder now, and we both knew it. "This one goes through me."

I Sang long, sure notes—ones that rang with mission and focus and higher calling. "You're a Fixer, Tameka. We don't do this."

She snorted, even as beads of sweat started to pop out on her face. "You're not just a Fixer, Lakisha Drinkwater —you're a human being. Trust your Talent, your brain, your heart, your digger-rock common sense."

I was. I gathered my notes to my chest, shaping them into something that would blow through the Dancer's net.

"Don't." Tameka held up both hands, the universal sign of surrender from a woman suddenly shaky on her feet. She met my gaze with eyes that weren't shaky at all. "You can do it, we both know that. But I don't think you want to."

Devan stepped up to her shoulder, crackling with energy entirely his own.

I seized every gram of Talent I had left. Looked away from the eyes of a woman who had chosen to live out the rest of her days as a blade of grass under a magic, dancing sky—and into the furious, pleading eyes of the man I loved.

And then, tortured, sad, and cracked—I let my Song go.

I couldn't do it. To her, or to him, or to what was left of my ravaged heart.

But there was another way to finish this that wouldn't require any Talent at all—and I'd even worn the right footwear. It was time to use my boots for the purpose they'd been designed for.

I fled.

22

I ROUNDED the corner of the bubble tunnel that funneled travelers into the main waiting area of Bromelain III's tiny spaceport, tired and cranky from my night sleeping on a hard bench. The waiting area wasn't very crowded—probably because the only ship picking people up today was a milk run through the outer colonies. It stopped often, dropping off necessities, raw materials, and the occasional passenger dumb enough to think the cheap fares were worth the snail's pace and lack of onboard amenities.

I wasn't nearly that dumb, but the planet three stops away had a bigger spaceport and an express flight to Corinthian Station. Once I made it that far, catching a tin can to Stardust Prime would be reasonably easy.

I got a better grip on my bag and looked around for anything resembling food. My stomach was already complaining about the lack of bacon.

It would have to get used to it—Stardust Prime didn't run to much pig.

"Hungry?" The voice at my shoulder held out a bright red apple.

I turned to stare at Janelle, clad in jeans, striped shirt, and a really dusty hat. She looked like she'd just jumped off a horse. "How the heck did you get in here?" This was a restricted area and the guys at Interplanetary customs tended to take their jobs pretty seriously. It was the main reason I'd slept on a bench.

She patted her pocket. "I have a ticket as of thirty minutes ago. Same flight as you."

Like hell she did. "I had to twist some serious arms to get a ride." Arms and a lot of drinks at the bar—spacers didn't tend to like passengers, no matter what rules their investors tried to set.

She grinned. "You're not related to the pilot."

No, but I'd happily strangle him. "I'm not looking for company."

"Yeah." She bit into the apple I hadn't taken. "Got that."

"How'd you even find me?"

"It's not rocket science—there aren't all that many ways to leave BroThree." She shrugged. "But apparently Tameka expected you to try days ago. A friend of hers has been keeping an eye on ship manifests."

Nobody freaking spied on Fixers. "Yesenia would bust her to deck swabbing for that."

"She could try."

I could feel a boatload of pissy anger rising and seriously considered just letting it fly at the top of my very well-trained lungs. A full-blown Singer temper tantrum would feel damn good right about now.

"So." Janelle hitched her bag a little higher up her shoulder. "Why are you headed to Haida Gant?"

I knew exactly nothing about my destination. "Because it's not here." I hated the bitter tones in my voice. "I'm leaving, tail between my legs."

"That's what Tameka figured."

That particular old lady had gotten in my way far too often in the past twenty-four hours. "I should have left a long time ago."

The woman who had somehow become a friend just stood beside me, munching on my damn apple. And every time she chewed, I got a little less angry and a little more sad.

I turned to face her while I still could. There was one thing she deserved to know before I hopped on a cubesat and never saw her again. "I need to go because I can't get this assignment finished, at least not the way they wanted me to. But as soon as I get back and report in, they're going to send someone who can." KarmaCorp didn't leave frayed ends hanging, especially on a mission that had gone as high up the bureaucratic chain as this one had.

She shrugged. "They can try."

"They'll make it happen." I reached out a hand and dropped it again, not remotely sure how to do this right. "You could make it happen first."

She raised a slow eyebrow. "Not gonna."

I flung mental curses at her hard, stubborn head. "You'd fit right in on a digger rock, you know that?"

She laughed. "I'll take that as a compliment."

I hadn't meant it as one.

She held out the bulgy bag she'd been carrying. "Apples and butter. Parting gifts from Tameka and me, just in case you keep being stupid and actually leave. She said your roommate would know what to do with them."

Ingredients for the best damn apple pie in the galaxy. Tee would be overjoyed. "I'm leaving even if I have to Sing the freaking solar winds myself."

She blinked. "You can do that?"

Not even kind of. "I won't need to. I've been on this planet for a week—the wind never stops blowing."

"We like it that way." Janelle looked out the window for a while, as patient as the grasslands she called home.

I tried one last time. "Give Devan a chance. You were thinking about going there anyhow, so do it."

She raised an eyebrow. "No."

I resisted the urge to punch her in the nose—barely. "You don't know what a Fixer can do if she's really trying. Let it be your choice, not some dumb flatlander's."

"I won't bother to tell you how badly you're underestimating Devan," said Janelle quietly. "And I won't kick at you for thinking so little of our friendship, because I don't think your head is on very straight right now. But I will say this. KarmaCorp has asked two Fixers to intervene in this, and in the end, neither of you were willing to do it. Doesn't that tell you something?"

I stared. She knew about Tameka's refusal? "The guy in charge of your planet is pushing for this. So are a bunch of StarReaders and who knows how many other bureaucrats." I didn't give a shit about Ears Only anymore. "You can't fight everyone."

"Those are all crappy reasons for me to fall in love with Devan Lovatt."

Sometimes it took no reasons at all.

"And besides, this is really simple." She pitched what was left of the apple at a compost tube, grinned, and slung her arm through mine. "I'm not nearly dumb enough to get between whatever is going on with him and you."

The woman was strong enough to drag a horse. "He can't be mine."

"I think you might be too late on that."

I planted my feet and pulled us both to a stop. "I have a flight to catch."

"Not anymore, you don't. And if you're ornery, I can ask my second cousin the pilot to make it official." She somehow had both our feet moving again. "We'll go have some decent breakfast. With bacon. And then I'm going to duct tape you and that idiot Devan Lovatt into a room together and see what happens."

I blinked. "You can't do that."

"Bets?" She was quick-marching us into the egress tunnel. "I may not be a fancy Fixer or anything like that, but here on BroThree we're pretty good at dealing with stupid."

"And you think sticking me in a room with him will fix that?" My voice squeaked an octave higher than it should be.

"It will fix something." Her voice carried unmistakable amusement—and more than a little ribald humor.

I scowled. "What's so damn funny?"

"You came here to mess with my knickers." She grinned. "You ended up getting yours in a twist instead, and I'm petty enough to get a kick out of that. Poetic justice and all."

I yanked us both to a stop again.

This time, Janelle let go and reached into her bag. "Before you're a total nimwit, there's something you need to read."

I looked at the small, white, folded thing she held out and took a giant step backward. I'd faced radioactive waste more bravely.

Her hand didn't waver. "Tameka sent a message for you."

My fingers reached out, digits that belonged to someone else in a parallel universe.

The message was written on rough, handmade paper decorated with small flowers and something that might be grass stems. And covered in a slashing, opinionated scrawl that I could barely read.

I squinted and held the paper up to the light.

You run because you seek freedom, child of the rocks. Stand and claim it. There is so much more of it available than what you have dared to reach for.

There is a wound in you that matches the one you found in Devan's heart—the wound of a person who has done what they needed to survive, and done it very well. You began to heal him, and you did it with great love and even greater courage.

I wonder if you dare to do the same for yourself.

Tameka

P.S. I almost had to sit on Roland's knee to get the butter, so take good care of it. And say hello to your Tee for me. She is formidable and kind, and I imagine she is a wonderful friend.

My eyes blurred. Very carefully, I folded the paper up and slipped it in my pocket next to my travel voucher to Haida Gant. I swallowed hard, let go one very wavery breath, and looked at Janelle. "Do you know what she wrote?"

She shrugged, a little hesitant. "More or less."

"She's an interfering old woman."

"She is." Janelle put both hands in her pockets and started walking slowly down the egress tunnel again.

I kept pace beside her, well aware she wasn't dragging me anymore.

"I don't have her power, or her wisdom. But I have some words for you, just like you had some for me." She walked a few more quiet, measured steps and pushed open a door out into the dry, fresh air of Bromelain III. "Out here, it's okay to reach for what you want."

I felt anguish rising up from the very bottoms of my feet. "I have no idea what I want."

The ends of her mouth tipped up. "Like hell you don't."

She held out a hand, pointing to Nijinsky hovering nearby. And dangled the access card.

I took a deep breath. And reached.

23

I WALKED through the massive front gates of the Lovatt compound and reined in the insistent instinct to run back out. Janelle would only make good on her duct-tape threat if I did that, and she'd probably have Nijinsky's owner standing right behind her.

No, that wasn't fair. I was no cog this time. This choice was entirely mine.

I stumbled across the outer courtyard and into the cool hallways, well aware of just how many times during my stay I'd arrived in this kind of shape. My Song careened around inside me, a confused, knotted mess that had been so clear only ten minutes ago. I knew the shape of what I needed to do, but nothing in the music forming as I had flown had prepared me for dodging bustling staff people or keeping a wary eye open for Evgenia or my stomach's very loud appeal for one last plate of bacon.

Real life is so much messier than they ever tell you.

I squared my shoulders—this was no different than

digging a mine. There were a lot of details and most of them mattered, but there was only one goal. Dig.

I needed to dig my way through to Devan. I could worry about what came next when I got there.

My Song's epic jangling soothed some—it understood having a purpose. I trekked through the hallowed halls, hiding from scrutiny where I could and using my Fixer identity as a shield when I couldn't. I was an honored guest here, or I would be until the higher-ups discovered just how close I'd come to running away in the dark of night with my tail between my legs—and that I'd come back.

I saw no signs of the lady of the house, even as I made my way into more private parts of the residence. Unfortunately, I saw no signs of the Inheritor Elect either.

My Song started its wild screeching runs again, traumatized by the loss of intention. I told it to go sit quietly in the corner with my bacon-craving stomach, and turned down a hallway at random.

Three more hallways, and the notes inside me had gotten frantic. Of course he wasn't here. He'd be at his stream, dangling his toes in the water, or flying Ophelia, or something else that would tend to that huge heart of his.

I spun around and started to run, heading for the nearest exit—and plowed straight into rock.

"Oof." Devan made a sound like a farting elephant as I landed on top of him, brain rattling in my skull and teeth contemplating doing the same. He wrapped one arm around me and touched the back of his head gingerly with the other hand. "Mom used to tell us not to run in the halls. That's never made sense until today."

I winced. "Shit, I'm so sorry. Does it hurt?"

"That depends." His eyes watched me. Intent. Careful. "Would you kiss it better?"

I would want to. So terribly much.

I met those eyes as best as I could, entirely uncertain what to say. The last time he'd seen me I'd been running too. He had no way of knowing that I'd changed directions.

He didn't move. I listened to the sound of his heart, beating under my ribs.

And knew it wasn't words I needed to find.

With what little bits of grace I had left, I levered myself off Devan Lovatt's chest, slid back enough that I no longer touched him, and sat, legs crossed and spine straight, in the first pose taught to all trainees. I closed my eyes, breathed in the air of the dusky hallway and exhaled again, knowing the winds of this place would carry some molecules of me to the far reaches of this planet.

And then I let my eyes seek Devan's face. "I would like to Sing for you."

He pushed himself up to sitting and mirrored my pose, watching me with those intense, careful eyes. "Okay."

I felt, more than heard, shadows scurrying in the background. And quailed. Last night had been very public. I needed this to be private.

He held up a palm. "Wait." He beckoned one of the

shadows, and they hurried off. Moments later, I could feel the hallway emptying.

"Thank you." My voice sounded husky to my ears, unused. I felt it echoing. We were alone now. I let my head tilt down and whispered a note of gratitude. It wasn't the majestic grasslands or a burbling stream—but it would do.

I could feel his eyes on me, watching.

"Tameka told me what you did for me." His voice sounded wary. Curious. Determined. "She said that if you came back, it would mean you had done the same thing for yourself."

Interfering old woman. "Something like that." I didn't really know what I had done just yet. I only knew that I was here—and I had something I needed to do.

I let my eyes slide shut and grounded, down through my skinsuit and the floor under my butt and the vibrations of this place to the heartbeat of the planet below. I shunted the skittering worry aside. I was here, and right now, here was all that mattered. There would be consequences for this choice, I knew that. I would pay them later.

I breathed—through my palms, my fingers, my nose, my spine. Let the hairs on my head tingle as I let it all flow upward.

And gathered my Song.

I looked into Devan's eyes, as deep and hard and intensely as I'd ever headed at any rock. And let the first notes rise in my throat.

There was no leaning in these ones, no influence. I was not a Fixer today.

The first note was creaking, wispy, and even a little off key. I watched him smile—a man who knew exactly what lived in that poor, misbegotten, utterly beautiful note. And offered him the rest.

Time folded, the way it always does when I go deepest. The music soared high and ran wild underground, floated on whispers and drilled into bedrock. I could feel my soul shaking. Steadying. Living. Breath, clarity, and utter presence—in the notes, and in the still, quiet spaces between them. With all the Talent and love I possessed, I put Lakisha Drinkwater out into the universe for one man to see.

And when I came back out again, quivering, feeling the last inaudible harmonics of my Song rippling out into the hallway, Devan's eyes were the first thing I saw.

The only thing I saw.

His fingertips brushed mine, as lightly as stardust. "What—?" He cleared his throat, a man struggling to find enough moisture to speak. "What was that?"

I smiled and pulled myself up straight. I would offer this to him without remorse, without regret. "I am a Singer, and that is my heart's Song." Something offered only rarely, because for the rest of my life, part of me would be walking the galaxy outside my body. It was the most precious thing I had to give.

His head bowed down, the pads of his fingers resting ever so gently under mine. "It was beautiful." A deep sigh, and then he looked so deeply into me that I nearly fractured. "You're beautiful."

It wasn't my face he was seeing now, I knew that. It was my Song. My soul. I let my hands stretch out over his, wanting to hold, knowing I couldn't.

I could only ask.

"Will you come see me?" It was an entirely selfish request—one full of hardship and entanglement and promises I couldn't keep. I frowned and dropped my hands, but never let my eyes leave his. "You should say no."

His smile dawned, twin moons coming up over a dark horizon. "I heard that from you once before."

I'd been right that time too. "I'm a Fixer, Devan. My life isn't my own." And even if it was, I had no business messing with a man who'd dumped himself onto Karma-Corp's radar. My job was to sand some of history's rough edges. I had a sneaking suspicion that Devan's job was to make it.

"Mine isn't entirely my own either." He drew in a long, full breath. "But enough of it is that I will say yes."

I closed my eyes and let my fingers touch his again. He would come, and I would Sing for him again.

And we would see what destiny would make of that.

24

SOME THINGS DIDN'T CHANGE JUST because you've traveled a thousand lightyears. I skulked down the walkways of KarmaCorp's headquarters on Stardust Prime, sticking to shadows as I made my way to the boss lady's office.

I'd come on the double from the spaceport, hoping to circumvent some of Yesenia's wrath by arriving before she expected me. Probably a lost cause—I'd been in transit for a week. Plenty long enough for her to have worked up a galaxy-sized storm, full of lots of space shrapnel.

All the better to shred me with. Yesenia didn't tolerate failure.

"Kish!"

Tee's hand reaching out from a dark doorway frayed what few nerves I had left. She yanked me into a storage closet, slammed the door behind us, and grabbed at my shoulders, hands frantic. "What the hell happened out there?"

Nothing I dared tell her. "I got back from assignment, I need to report in. End of story."

"Right." She scanned me up and down, one Grower in high dudgeon. "Tameka sent me a message. She said your heart would likely need tending."

That broke every kind of rule there was. "Gods, Tee —stay out of this, okay?" The last thing on earth I needed right now was the whole Lightbody family trying to come to my aid.

"Like hell." My best friend took two steps back and propped herself on the edge of a box, arms folded and eyes fierce. "Talk. Tameka wouldn't. I tried."

I knew just how hard Tee could try when she wanted to. I fingered the old Fixer's handwritten note, still in my pocket. It was much crumpled now from countless readings en route.

Trying to remember why I'd done this.

Because somewhere in the first leg of my flight home, I'd realized what I should have known before I'd ever invited Devan Lovatt to come visit—Yesenia could flick her fingers and keep him from setting foot within lightyears of me ever again. I'd been high on some heady combination of love, insanity, and bacon fumes if I'd managed to forget that for even an instant.

I looked over at my roommate, still shooting daggers from her perch on a box of supplies. "I don't even know where to start. How much do you know?"

"Nothing." She pursed her lips grimly. "There's not

even a whisper circulating here, and Tameka wouldn't tell me shit."

Tameka had done plenty just by contacting Tee in the first place—but it was far more astonishing that the rumor mill of Stardust Prime had nothing. "How can there not be whispers?"

"I don't know." She looked even grimmer now. "I don't like it, Kish."

She wasn't the only one. There were always rumors. Always, and Tee would have her hands in the thick of them. If there weren't, someone was doing a very thorough job of scrubbing them—and as far as I knew, only one person had that kind of reach.

Yesenia didn't want anyone to know I'd failed.

That scared me enough to get me talking. "I was supposed to make the Inheritor Elect of Bromelain III fall in love with one of his neighbors." I gulped. "I kind of fell in love with him instead."

Tee's face was a conundrum of empathy, fascination, and horror. "Oh, hell. Oh, no."

"It gets worse. He kind of fell in love with me too." Or he'd been well on his way, anyhow.

Horror won. Tee yanked me down onto a box beside her, her hands wrapping my face like she could protect me if she just held on tight enough. "What the hell did you do?"

"I left." I looked straight into her eyes and wondered if it was the last time I'd get to see them. Fixers in exile didn't get passes to Stardust Prime. "But first, I Sang for him. And I invited him to come visit me."

She turned sheet white. We both knew how bad this was. Three hundred years of history made very clear what happened when we didn't follow orders. There would be a calm, organized, very convincing cleanup of any nasty ripples—KarmaCorp didn't leave galactic messes. And I would spend the rest of my life chained to a pile of paperwork somewhere that would make Bromelain III look like the cradle of civilization.

Death by irrelevance.

And that's if I was lucky. The StarReaders would measure the consequences of my actions—they likely already had. And then KarmaCorp would do what it needed to do.

None of which would change what happened in Yesenia's office. I hadn't followed orders. Even if I hadn't changed the destiny of the universe one hair, she was still going to want my head.

Because I had taken the risk. Because I had dared to create ripples of my own making.

Tee was watching me carefully. "Tameka said she tried to stop you."

I hoped like hell she hadn't put that in her report to Yesenia. The choice had been mine, and the head rolling should be mine, too.

My roommate's voice had quieted. "She said you let her."

I looked down at the scratched floor under my feet. I couldn't lie to Tee—she knew exactly how much Talent I had and what I could do with it. "I shouldn't have."

"Hmm." She sounded almost bemused. "Do you know why you did?"

Because I hadn't wanted to see a proud legend reduced to gelatin. "Does it matter?"

"Yes," she said, so quietly I could barely hear her. "He must be an amazing man."

He was. But he wasn't the only reason my head was about to roll.

Because on day six in the tin can, I'd finally figured something else out. As much as my instincts for self-preservation wanted to believe otherwise, this assignment had changed me in ways that had nothing to do with Devan Lovatt.

Diggers do what they're told or they die. Fixers do what they're told—or someone else dies. Or at least that's what I'd convinced myself over the last fifteen years, with the thorough cooperation of the corporation I worked for. I had chosen to become a loyal cog, to imprint Karma-Corp's mission on my soul.

I had chosen to rebel in small ways—and bow down in large ones.

It wasn't hard to understand why. I'd crashed into the side of a mining asteroid before I was a week old, then been yanked out of that life because of something I could do with the notes of a song. My life was solid evidence that destiny happened to me—I didn't create it.

Until one small moment on a backwater planet when a different wind had blown at my back.

A moment that, no matter how much my boots were shaking now, I couldn't bring myself to regret. When I'd landed on Bromelain III, I'd believed that what I *did* mattered. Now I believed that *I* mattered. I was still flotsam—but I was a different kind of flotsam.

Or at least I would be until Yesenia was done with me.

I reached for my roommate's hands. "Keep your family out of this, okay?" The Lightbodys were a force to be reckoned with on this planet, but they were no match for Yesenia on a tear.

"Not going to happen," said Tee softly.

It damn well was, even if I had to throw myself out of a space chute to make sure of it. "Delay them at least." That would buy me some time to sacrifice whatever body parts Yesenia might take as compensation for the shit storm I'd landed on her desk.

"Go." She pulled open the storage room door and laid a hand on my arm as I moved to leave. "Iggy and Raven will be waiting at our place."

Friends at my back. "Circling the wagons, huh?"

"Yeah." She slid her hand down my arm and squeezed my fingers again. "Something like that."

I kept my face as calm as I could, tossing her the bag I'd been carrying as I stood to go. "Apples and butter. I'll be there in time for the pie."

I didn't meet her eyes. I knew neither of us believed it.

25

BEAN LOOKED up from her desk as I walked into the outer rings of Yesenia's sanctum. "Hey, Kish—how was the trip?"

I squinted at her innocent face. "You haven't heard?" All gossip on Stardust Prime routed itself through this office before it went anywhere else. Tee hadn't been kidding.

Her eyebrows shot up. "No. What am I supposed to have heard?"

She'd find out soon enough. I nodded at the boss lady's door. "Has her head started steaming yet?"

Bean's eyes slammed shut and then opened again very slowly, as if I might be some kind of hallucination. "No. She just ordered waffles and a fruit bowl for break-fast. What the heck is going on?"

I stared, suspicious and confused. Yesenia's eating habits were the stuff of Fixer legend—the woman's food consumption totally tracked her moods. Waffles and a fruit bowl sure didn't sound like hurricane-level fury. "Seriously? She's not in there muttering inventive death threats under her breath?"

"I don't think so." Bean shook her head slowly. "She was here early, chatty when we ran through her morning agenda, and she's got some pretty Ethulian flute music playing, or she did last time I was in there."

Yesenia's music consumption also tracked her moods. "No Rachmaninoff?" Even a second-year trainee knew what that meant. RUN.

Bean stopped bouncing on the exercise ball she used as a chair. "If you don't fill me in right now, I will make sure you get assigned to every trainee introductory tour until the end of time." She fixed me with one of the stares that had earned her the job as the boss lady's gatekeeper. "And that will just be for starters."

That was a nuclear warhead kind of threat. I opened my mouth, prepared to give up my mother, my secret chocolate stash, and the keys to the vault on Meridian Five—but not the details of my assignment—when Yesenia's door slid open. "You will learn the outcome of Journeywoman Drinkwater's trip in due time, Lucinda. In the meantime, do you have the files for the new graduates ready? I'd like to look at them again before we match them with their first assignments."

Any other assistant would have taken that as a very pointed message to get back to work. Bean just tilted her head slightly, dreadlocks shaking, and watched the two of us with avid interest.

Another reason she was the boss lady's gatekeeper—Lucinda Coffey might be the only person on the planet who wasn't scared of Yesenia Mayes. No one had any idea why that was the case. Bean had just shown up one day and turned herself into the most essential person on Stardust Prime.

"Journeywoman?"

By the tone of Yesenia's voice, she'd been standing there indicating her door for more than the last nanosecond.

I gulped and moved my feet with dispatch—unlike Bean, I was plenty scared of the woman who ran all the parts of KarmaCorp I'd ever known.

I headed straight for my usual spot on the carpet, square in front of her desk. "Ready to report." I might be nervy as a snake in a volcano, but I damn well didn't intend to cower.

Yesenia slowly made her way behind the desk and took a seat in the towering black chair that trainees were occasionally dumb enough to call her throne. "I've been awaiting your arrival. I appreciate you coming to me so quickly."

Her words carried no hint of whether she was about to rip off my head and feed it to a wormhole, or just put me on dustpan duty for the rest of my natural life. "I failed in my mission. I wanted you to know immediately." A foolish gesture—transmissions traveled far faster than human bodies in space. She likely already knew every last sordid detail.

"That's an interesting characterization." She tilted

her chair back slightly. "Why don't you tell me your version of events and then we'll decide whether you've tarnished your record, shall we?"

I tried not to stare and failed utterly. She was toying with me. The woman could be brutal, but I'd never seen her be cruel. I proceeded, stuttering, wondering whether she'd come up with a fate worse than wormholes. "I was sent to Bromelain III to arrange a mutually interested romantic relationship between the Inheritor Elect and a woman from a family of significant local stature. That outcome was not accomplished."

She inclined her head slightly. "I hear Devan and Janelle were not overly cooperative."

That wasn't the kind of thing that was supposed to matter. "Local support is not required for successful assignment completion."

Yesenia's left eyebrow rose a very controlled centimeter. "How long are you going to stand there and quote me the manual that I wrote, Journeywoman?"

Oops. That was definitely pissed-off boss lady. "I'm done."

"Good." She sighed and shook her head. "I know you weren't pleased to have this particular assignment in the first place. Would you like to hear why I sent you?"

Several very cranky replies popped into my head, side by side with the jaw-dropping astonishment of the boss lady offering to explain herself. A week in a flying tin can never has me at my best. A week of contemplating probable career suicide and the idiocy of pining for a man

I would probably never see again while in that tin can had left me riding the thin edge of insanity.

I did, however, have enough remnants left to keep my mouth shut.

Yesenia stood, opened a chill box on her desk, and pulled out a shimmering glass bowl of fruit. "Here, it looks like you could use this more than I can."

I kept my hands behind my back. The exotic fruit was worth a week of my salary, and the handblown Venusian glass it sat in probably ran a hundred times that. "No, thank you."

"Journeywoman." The bowl landed on my side of the desk with a decided thunk. "Sit down, shut up, and eat. Now."

Shit. I sat. And after one more death glare from the other side of the desk, picked up the spoon. "Thank you."

"Better." Yesenia sat down and watched like a hawk as I took one small bite and then another.

Even a week's worth of pent-up terror couldn't make this taste like sawdust. I felt my idiot tongue revel in the bits of mango and pineapple and something that tasted like honey, and tried not to puke it back up.

If this was a condemned person's last meal, it was a worthy one.

It wasn't until I'd let the last spoonful slide down my throat that the woman on the other side of the desk spoke up again. "I sent you because you're one of my most creative Fixers." Her face could have given an ice sculpture a run for its money. "Although I must say that I didn't count on Tameka giving that particular quality of yours a good, hard push."

I was slightly stoned on mango and utterly lost. "I don't understand."

She frowned and looked at a place on the wall just over my right shoulder. "My job is not as easy as most of you think it is, Singer. We have very good men and women evaluating the energies of the universe, the places where the Talents of a Fixer might shift outcomes for the greater good."

Any first-year trainee knew that. "And our job is to do the mission as assigned."

"Correct." She looked squarely at me again. "What you don't know is that often the directives those good men and women issue are not straightforward. There are nuances, difficulties, gray areas. And in the case of this assignment, sometimes more than one possible desirable outcome."

That definitely wasn't something they told the first-year trainees. I stared at her, completely horrified. She was sounding like Tameka Boon.

"You wonder why we don't tell you."

I shook my head slowly. "No." I could feel the answer congealing in my gut. "It would make us less certain, less likely to act with clarity and conviction." It would make our Talents as wobbly as all hell.

I could still hear the sound of mine rending.

"For most, yes." She was studying me very carefully. "Fixers are human beings, and most human beings prefer a clear direction to follow."

My neurons had all chittered to a disoriented stop.

"Some don't." Yesenia's tone was dispassionate, almost clinical. "Those who don't are often our brightest and our best."

Somewhere inside my brain of ice, comprehension landed. "Like Tameka."

"Yes. What you as trainees learn of her is limited, and that is done at my directive. I don't need a herd of Tameka Boons to manage." She paused, an enigmatic look in her eyes. "But I do need a few. You have it in you to become one of them, Journeywoman. See that you do."

I stared, shocked to the rock-bottom soles of my feet. "I'm a fifth-year Fixer who royally screwed up her assignment. I'm nothing like Tameka."

"She doesn't agree with you." Yesenia said the next words as if they tasted slightly bitter. "And neither do I."

I'd seen a miner who'd been inside a tunnel blast once. I was pretty sure I knew how he felt.

"Let me speak clearly, Singer." Yesenia laid her hands on her desk. "This mission was the result of directives from the highest levels. It was quite clear that Devan Lovatt would be a major force in this quadrant one day, and also that there was value in encouraging his heart to open to a key relationship at this point in his life." She inclined her head slightly. "The directives were much less clear on who that should be."

I couldn't stop staring. "You sent me to put him together with Janelle."

She nodded crisply. "It is the outcome that the Star-Readers anticipated to be most likely."

I could hear it—the single note that she was clearly allowing me to hear. "You didn't agree with them."

"I am not always quite as certain as they are. I have some familiarity with strong-willed young people and the difficulty of predicting who they will become."

My mind was jibbering, trying to take in the utter annihilation of the world as I knew it. And then the full, immediately relevant import of Yesenia's words sank in.

"You expected this?" My astonishment was the size of a supernova and growing. "You sent me to Bromelain III knowing this would happen?"

She inclined her head slightly. "It was one of the possibilities."

That was insane. "I'm a Fixer. He's a man who will have to navigate a dozen bureaucrats before he can even enter inner-planet space." Never mind the shoes he would be filling one day.

"Not all of us choose easy paths, Singer." Her face gave nothing away. "You grew up digging holes in the side of a deep-space rock. I imagine you would find an easy life's journey rather boring."

This assignment had taken every possible crazy turn. At this point, I was just hanging on by my fingernails and trying not to die.

"I have one last thing for you." She reached behind her and lifted up a small box. "Emelio Lovatt couriered this to my attention. The accompanying message from his wife indicates that you would know what to do with it." She pushed the box across the desk and lifted the lid. "She also instructed me to make sure that you accept it."

I gawked at the kilo stack of shrink-wrapped bacon. It would have cost a king's ransom to send via galactic messenger. I looked at Yesenia, entirely stupefied. "Why on earth would they send me this?"

"You're not usually so dense, Journeywoman Drinkwater." The corners of her mouth hinted at what might almost be a smile. "I believe it is their way of telling you that they approve."

I stared, every molecule of my brain totally fried.

"Go, Singer. You've got work to do." Yesenia's tone was back to brusque and businesslike. "And if a certain young man from Bromelain III is ever in need of a visitor pass, I will instruct Lucinda to aid him in any way necessary."

I gaped. Bean could make anything happen. "You're not dropping me down a wormhole?"

"Not today." That hint of a smile was back. "Don't make me regret it."

I stumbled out of her office, the implications of her words racing through my mind and soul, setting fire to every neuron they touched.

I was not going to die today.

I was going to eat apple pie and bacon and hug my friends.

Yesenia had just given KarmaCorp's tacit blessing to a romance between a Fixer and an Inheritor Elect. Which meant the StarReaders had too.

I had made the choices of a renegade—and not been branded as one.

And I would see Devan again.

KEEP READING the KarmaCorp series with *Grower's Omen*, which is Tee's story, complete with life-changing potions, a crisis of faith, and a renegade tree.